Edward Everett

The Life of George Washington

Edward Everett

The Life of George Washington

ISBN/EAN: 9783337056353

Printed in Europe, USA, Canada, Australia, Japan

Cover: Foto ©Raphael Reischuk / pixelio.de

More available books at **www.hansebooks.com**

THE LIFE

OF

GEORGE WASHINGTON.

BY

EDWARD EVERETT.

NEW YORK:

SHELDON AND COMPANY.

BOSTON: GOULD AND LINCOLN.

1860.

RIVERSIDE, CAMBRIDGE:
STEREOTYPED AND PRINTED BY H. O. HOUGHTON.

PREFACE.

THE enterprising proprietors of the "Encyclopædia Britannica" requested the late Lord MACAULAY to prepare the article on "Washington," for the new Edition of that Work now in course of publication. His other engagements prevented his complying with their request, and thinking also that it would, on some accounts, be desirable that the memoir of Washington should be written by a countryman, he advised the Messrs. BLACK to apply to me. This they did in the month of March, 1859, expressing the wish that the article should be furnished to them in Edinburgh, in the month of October last. Though much occupied with previous engagements, and otherwise not favorably situated for cheerful mental effort, I thought it my duty to comply with the request of the Messrs. BLACK, regretting, however, that the time allowed me — besides constant interruptions — was too short to admit of careful research among the original materials for a life of Washington.

In fact, I feel that some apology is due to the public, for attempting to compress into the narrow compass of a volume like this a career like that of Washington, which has been so fully treated in the great national works of MARSHALL, SPARKS, and IRVING. It will, however, I think, be generally felt to have been desirable, that a comprehensive memoir of our illustrious Countryman should be prepared by an American writer, for a work like the " Encyclopædia Britannica," and a republication in this country follows as a matter of course. The purpose for which the memoir was written will, I trust, sufficiently account for the necessary condensation of the narrative; for the omission of many facts of importance, and for the superficial statement of others; as also for the occasional mention of what is familiar to every American, but which may need explanation to the European reader.

The historical materials of the following pages have been mainly derived from the standard works already alluded to, in which is contained everything of importance authentically known of the life and career of Washington. Diligent search among official papers and private letters will no doubt throw further light on matters of detail, especially as far as his domestic life is concerned; but it is hardly to be expected that anything will be added to our knowledge of important events. To Mr. SPARKS I am under especial obligations. No one can have occasion to write or to speak on the life of Washington, however compendiously, without finding constant occasion to repeat the acknowledgment of Mr. IRVING, who justly places him "among the greatest benefactors of our national literature."

I regret that the valuable work of Mr. BENSON J. LOSSING, entitled "Mount Vernon and its Associations," was not published till the following memoir was nearly completed, and it was consequently not in my power to make as much use as I could have wished of the stores of information contained in it. The same remark applies to the "Recollections and Memoirs of Washington," by the late Mr. G. W. PARKE CUSTIS, of which the excellent edition by Mr. LOSSING appeared too late to render me the assistance I might otherwise have derived from it.

In what I have said of the important topic of President WASHINGTON's "Farewell Address," I have followed the footsteps, at however great a distance, of the Hon. HORACE BINNEY, in his late exhaustive treatise on that subject; which seems to me to put to rest the hitherto existing uncertainty as to the preparation of that most important State-paper.

Although the plan of the following pages did not admit of great detail as to the private life of Washington, I could not forbear to narrate at length the incidents of the closing scene, as minutely described by an eye-witness. The nature of the disease of which Washington died, and its professional treatment by the attending physicians, having been sometimes drawn in question, it is with much satisfaction that I am able to lay before the reader, in the Appendix, a paper on that subject, written at my request, by my honored friend, Dr. JAMES JACKSON, the venerable head of his profession in this city.

I have also, through the kindness of Mr. JOHN A. WASHINGTON, procured from the archives of the Court in Fairfax County a copy of the official inventory of General WASHINGTON's personal estate. A copy of Mrs. WASHINGTON's Will has also been kindly furnished me from the same quarter. These documents will be found in the Appendix. They have never, I believe, been published.

I cannot close this preface without alluding to the melancholy tidings which have reached this country, within a few days, of the premature decease of the most brilliant writer of the age, perhaps of any age of English literature, — at whose suggestion the preparation of the following memoir was proposed to me by the publishers of the "Encyclopædia Britannica." Great as are the losses sustained by science and letters in Europe and America during the year 1859, the death of Lord MACAULAY is, in some respects, the greatest. Of the other illustrious persons who have been taken from us in the course of the year, some, as HUMBOLDT, HALLAM, and IRVING, had attained advanced years, and nobly completed the work given them to do. PRESCOTT, though leaving his last great work half written, leaves with it three completed histories, either of which would suffice for a reputation. MACAULAY, at a time of life which, in the course of nature, admitted many years of added labor, has been called away in the midst of the triumphant prosecution of his great enterprise. While the volumes already given to the world will go down to the latest

posterity as one of the most valuable
contributions to the literature of the English language, how keenly must we not
regret, that they form at best but a moi-
ety of the work, which might have been
confidently expected from his wondrous
pen! With what sorrow must we not
reflect, that the talent which could clothe
with the interest of romance a period of
English history not usually regarded as
the most inviting; that stores of information, collected by a memory of truly miraculous grasp, often from sources the
most obscure and distant, and arranged
with matchless skill, should be lost to us
forever, and this at the time when they
were most successfully employed for the
admiration of the reading world! Absolutely identifying himself with the scenes
he described, and mingling with fervor,
though under the guidance of laborious
research, in the great contentions of the

times, it was scarcely possible that he should fall into no errors of judgment, and never form a mistaken estimate of character. One such has been keenly felt in this country. But his work owes some of its highest qualities to that earnestness of conviction and warmth of feeling, which may, in the manner alluded to, have occasionally warped his judgment.

But admirable as he was as a writer, Lord MACAULAY was still more admirable as a man. His principles were liberal, his emotions generous, his manners affable, his life exemplary, his morals pure. The splendor of his page was, if possible, excelled by the brilliancy of his conversation. His personal intercourse was a perpetual feast of rational pleasure. The world admired the magnificence of his rhetoric, and contemplated with equal delight and wonder the profusion with which he poured forth the stores of his memory, gathered from the literature of every language and every country. Those who knew him loved him for his amiable personal qualities; for the unaffected meekness with which he bore his transcendent honors; for the sunny cheerfulness of his disposition, and the generous warmth of his heart. I cannot but reflect with melancholy satisfaction on the many happy hours passed in his society during four years of intimate acquaintance, and on the proofs of friendly regard with which he honored me to the very last days of his life.

EDWARD EVERETT.

Boston, 25th January, 1860.

CONTENTS.

CHAPTER IV.

CHAPTER V.

CHAPTER VI.

CHAPTER VII.

CHAPTER VIII.

APPENDIX.

No. I.

No. II.

No. III.

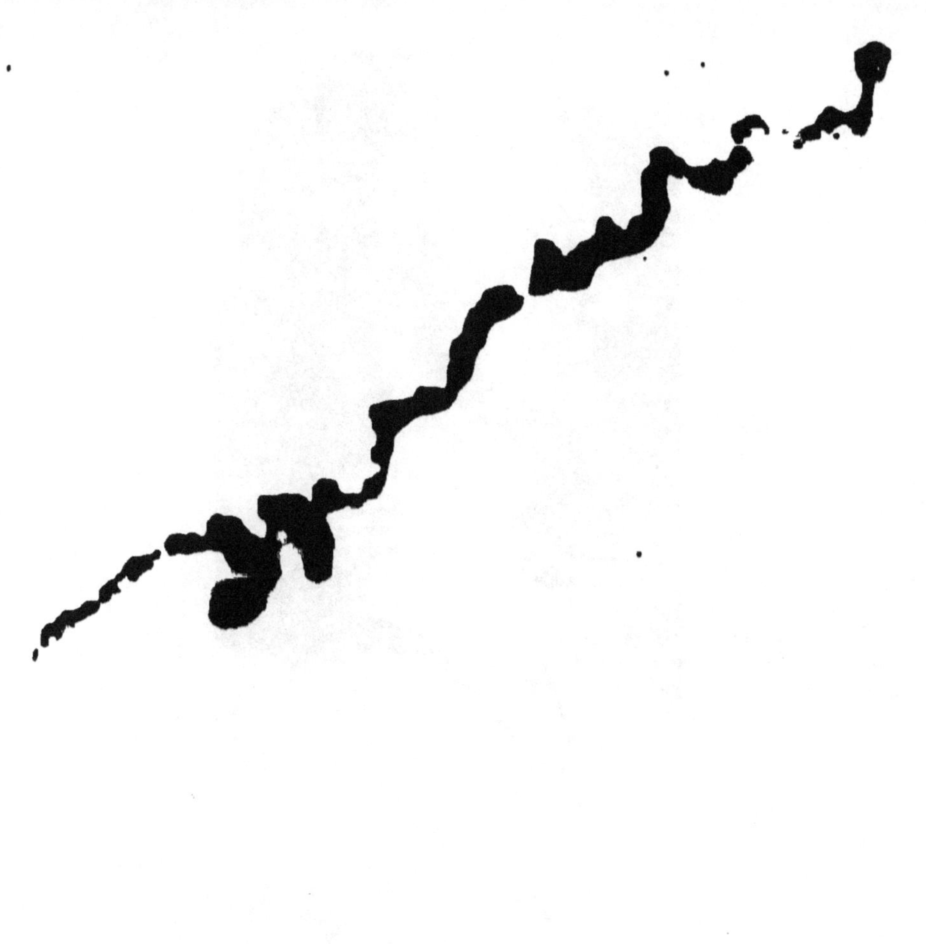

GEORGE WASHINGTON.

CHAPTER I.

In the family record contained in a Bible which belonged to the mother of Washington, and which is now in the possession of George Washington Bassett, of Hanover county, Virginia, who married a grandniece of Washington, the following entry is found:—

"George Washington, son to Augustine and Mary his wife, was born y[e] 11th day of February 173½ about ten in the morning, and was baptized the 3d of April following; Mr. Beverly Whiting and Captain Christopher Brooks, godfathers, and Mrs. Mildred Gregory godmother."

GEORGE WASHINGTON was accordingly born on the 22d of February, 1732, New Style, in the county of Westmoreland, in the parish of Washington, (so called from the family, whose seat it had been for three generations,) on Pope's Creek, a small tributary to the Potomac, and at the distance of about half a mile from its junction with that river. The house in which he was born was destroyed before the American Revolution, but a stone with a suitable inscription was placed upon the spot a few years since, by the late George Washington Parke Custis, the grandson of Mrs. Washington. This spot has lately been ceded to the State of Virginia.

The County of Westmoreland, famous

as the birthplace not only of Washington but of several other eminent persons, — such as Richard Henry Lee, who moved the resolution for declaring Independence in the Congress at Philadelphia in 1776; his three brothers, Thomas, Francis, and Arthur, and his kinsman, General Henry Lee, all distinguished in their day; James Monroe, the fifth President of the United States; and Bushrod Washington, a nephew of the General and a Justice of the Supreme Court, — lies between the Potomac and Rappahannoc rivers, in what is called the northern neck of Virginia. Notwithstanding the notoriety of the facts, a statement is sometimes made in British publications, and has been repeated by a respectable writer within the past year, (1858,) that George Washington was born in England.*

* The Editor of the *Cornwallis Papers*. The error was corrected in an *erratum*.

Augustine Washington, the father of the General, was twice married. His first wife was Jane Butler, by whom he had three sons and a daughter, namely, Butler, who died in infancy, Lawrence, Augustine, and Jane, the last-named of whom also died in childhood. His second wife was Mary Ball, to whom he was married on the 6th of March, 1730. By this marriage he had six children, namely, GEORGE, Betty, Samuel, John Augustine, Charles, and Mildred, the last of whom died in infancy.

George Washington was the great-grandson of John Washington, who, with a brother named Lawrence, emigrated to Virginia in 1657. They were great-grandsons of Lawrence Washington, sometime Mayor of Northampton, and the first lay proprietor of the manor of Sulgrave, in Northamptonshire, which was granted to him in 1538. Their eldest brother, Sir William Washington, married a half-sister of

George Villiers, the famous Duke of Buckingham. This connection indicates, if it did not cause, a leaning of the family toward the Royal side in the civil wars. Another of the name, Sir Henry Washington, a relative though not a brother, signalized himself by his persevering gallantry in sustaining the siege of Worcester against the Republican forces. Of the two brothers who came to Virginia, Lawrence had been a student at Oxford; John had resided on an estate at South Cave in Yorkshire, which gave rise to an erroneous tradition among his descendants, that their ancestor came from the North of England.

There is no doubt that the politics of the family determined the two brothers John and Lawrence to emigrate to Virginia, that colony being the favorite resort of the Cavaliers, during the government of Cromwell, as New England was the retreat of the Puritans, in the period which preceded the Commonwealth. John Washington and his brother took up lands and became successful planters in Virginia. The former, soon after his arrival, rose to the rank of Colonel in the Indian wars, and gave his name to the parish in which he lived. He married Ann Pope, by whom he had two sons, Lawrence and John, and a daughter. Lawrence, the oldest son, married Mildred Warner, of the neighboring county of Gloucester, and had three children, John, Augustine, and Mildred. The second son, Augustine, was the father of GEORGE WASHINGTON.

About fifty years before the emigration from England, the family removed from Sulgrave to Brington (near Althorpe), in Northamptonshire. The name of Washington may still be seen on the gravestones in the church of that and other parishes in the county. The original grantee of

Sulgrave was probably born at Warton, in Lancashire, where his father is known to have lived. In the next generation after the emigration to America, another of the family, perhaps a brother, passed to the Continent and established himself in Bavaria, where the descendants, bearing the family name and somewhat resembling General George Washington in personal appearance, are still found.

It may be mentioned as a somewhat striking fact, and one I believe not hitherto adverted to, that the families of Washington and Franklin, — the former the great leader of the American Revolution, the latter not second to any of his patriotic associates, — were established for several generations in the same central county of Northamptonshire, and within a few miles of each other; the Washingtons, at Brington and Sulgrave, belonging to the landed gentry of the county and in the

great civil war supporting the royal side;
the Franklins, at the village of Ecton, living on the produce of a farm of thirty acres and the earnings of their trade
as blacksmiths, and espousing, — some of
them at least, and the father and uncle of
Benjamin Franklin among the number, —
the principles of the non-conformists. Their
respective emigrations, germs of great
events in History, took place, — that of
John Washington, the great-grandfather
of George, in 1657, to loyal Virginia; —
that of Josiah Franklin, the father of
Benjamin, about the year 1685, to the
metropolis of Puritan New England.

The genealogy of George Washington
is a matter of greater importance to the
memory of his ancestors than to his own;
he throws back far greater glory than he
can inherit. Nevertheless, it may be a
matter of curiosity to note, that the family and name are traced by genealogists

to the twelfth century, and to the county of Durham. Among those who held manorial estates in that region, in the period succeeding the Norman Conquest, was William de Hertburn, so called from his estate, probably the modern Hartburn on the Tees. This estate was exchanged by him for that of Wessyngton, and with it the family name, which afterwards passed into Washington. From this person thus designated, the family of Washington, in its various branches, and now widely spread in England, on the Continent of Europe, and in the United States, is descended. For further details on this subject, — for which the limits of this work afford no room, — the reader is referred to the Appendix to the first volume of Mr. Sparks's admirable edition of the "Writings of Washington," and to the first volume of his Life, by the late honored and lamented

Nestor of American literature. General Washington's own feelings on the genealogy of his family are intimated in his answer to a letter from Sir Isaac Heard, Garter King at Arms, in 1792. Sir Isaac having addressed a letter to Washington, at that time President of the United States, making inquiry about his genealogy, the President, in his reply, says: "This is a subject to which I confess I have paid very little attention. My time has been so much occupied in the busy and active scenes of life from an early period of it, that but a small portion of it could have been devoted to researches of this nature, even if my inclination or particular circumstances should have prompted to the inquiry."

Shortly after the birth of George Washington, his father removed his family from the county of Westmoreland to that of Stafford, and established himself on an estate upon the eastern bank of the Rappahannoc River, opposite Fredericksburg, where he died in 1743, leaving a valuable landed property to his widow and five children. To his oldest son, Lawrence, he gave an estate near Hunting Creek, on the Potomac River, afterwards called Mount Vernon; to George, the oldest son of the second marriage, the estate opposite Fredericksburg; and to each of the other sons a plantation of six or seven hundred acres;—the income of the whole being left within the control of the mother, till the sons respectively should come of age.

The mother was a woman of superior intelligence and energy, and ruled her family and household with a firm hand. The means of education at that time, compared with the present day, were scanty in all the Anglo-American colonies, but especially at the South, where a larger portion of the inhabitants lived on their landed estates, and the population was less compact. The sons of affluent planters were sometimes sent "home," as it was called, and placed at the English schools and universities, and afterwards at the inns of court; but for others, who for any cause were unable to avail themselves of these advantages, the instruction to be had at the local schools in the Southern colonies did not extend beyond the ordinary branches of an English education. George Washington was taught reading, writing, book-keeping, and at a later period surveying; an important occupation at that time, being liberally compensated, and affording facilities for finding out and entering valuable ungranted lands in the almost boundless wilderness, which lay west of the settled parts of the country. Some of the manuscript books kept by him at school are still preserved.

They are marked by neatness, method, skill in the use of figures, in the construction of tables, and in the delineation of plans;—in a word, by the display of the favorite tastes which he carried through life, and manifested in the business details of military and civil affairs of importance.

According to still existing traditions, he evinced in his boyhood the military taste, which seems to have been hereditary in his family. The self-elected but willingly obeyed leader of his comrades, he formed them into companies for their juvenile battles. His early repute for veracity and justice, with his athletic prowess beyond his years, made him the chosen umpire of their disputes. He wrestled, leaped, ran, threw the bar, and rode with the foremost. A spot is still pointed out, where, in his boyhood, he threw a stone across the Rappahannoc;

he was proverbially strong of arm; in manhood he had one of the largest hands ever seen;* and he was through life a bold and graceful horseman.

Among his manuscripts still in existence, there is one, written under thirteen years of age, which deserves to be mentioned as containing striking indications of early maturity. The piece referred to is entitled "Rules of Civility and Decent Behavior in Company and Conversation." These rules are written out in the form of maxims, to the number of one hundred and ten. "They form," says Mr. Sparks, who gives a considerable specimen of them, "a minute code of regulations for building up the habits of morals and manners and good conduct in very

* The late Hon. Timothy Pickering, who was Secretary of State under Washington and the elder President Adams, said, in my hearing, that General Washington was the only man whom he ever knew, that had a larger hand than himself.

young persons." Whether they were taken in a body from some manual of education, or compiled by Washington himself from various books, or framed from his own youthful observation and reflection, is unknown. The first is, perhaps, the more probable supposition. If compiled by a lad under thirteen, and still more if the fruit of his own meditations, they would constitute a most extraordinary example of early prudence and thoughtfulness. Some of the rules, which form a part of this youthful code of manners and morals, had their influence over Washington and gave a complexion to his habits, through life.

Washington's early education did not extend beyond his own language, nor was that taught grammatically either in England or this country a hundred years ago. The grammatical rules of the English tongue were first learned from the study of the Latin language. Washington gave some attention to the French in after-life, when the armies of Count de Rochambeau were placed under his command; but he never attempted to speak or write it. By long practice, attentive reading of good authors, and scrupulous care in the preparation of his letters and other compositions, he acquired a correct and perspicuous English style.

While he was still at school, a project was formed by some of his relatives and friends, which, if it had taken effect, would have changed the entire course of his life. His oldest brother, Lawrence, had been an officer in the war lately waged to avenge the loss of "Captain Jenkins's ears;" he had served as a captain on the Spanish Main, and formed friendly relations with General Wentworth and Admiral Vernon. Observing the military turn of his brother George, he naturally thought he should promote his advancement in life by placing him in the British service. A midshipman's warrant was obtained for him, no doubt through Admiral Vernon's interest; but the prophetic heart of the mother rebelled at the last moment, and the project was abandoned, although his luggage, it is said, had been sent on board a ship of war lying in the Potomac.

Washington is unquestionably to be added to the list of eminent men whose characters have been moulded by a mother's influence. The control of their children's property, devolved upon her by the will of her husband, shows his confidence in her discretion and energy; and tradition represents her as a woman of vigorous character, fully equal to the trust. The modest dwelling in Fredericksburg, in which she passed the latter part of her life, is still standing, and, in its unpretending style and dimensions, forms a striking contrast with the ambitious, half-finished monument over her grave. She educated her children in habits of frugality, diligence, and virtue. Books, at that time, were few; — the luxuries, not the daily food of the mind, even among persons of fortune and leisure. With those in narrower circumstances, the range of reading did not extend much beyond the Bible, manuals of devotion, the sermons of some standard divine, and books of practical piety. Among the few books belonging to the elder generation, and still preserved at Mount Vernon, is a well-worn copy of Sir Matthew Hale's "Contemplations," a volume which had belonged to George Washington's father, and in which the names of his two wives, Jane and Mary, are written, each in her own hand-writing, on the blank page. It would not be difficult to point out in the character

of Washington some practical exemplifica-
tion of the maxims of the Christian life,
as laid down by that illustrious magis-
trate.

It is worthy of remark, that, although
he had not himself received a college
education, Washington entertained decided
opinions of its utility. He appropriated
the shares in the Potomac and James
River Canal, presented to him by the
legislature of Virginia, for the endowment of collegiate institutions, and recom-
mended, in his last annual message to
Congress, the foundation of a national
university at the seat of the general
government.

CHAPTER II.

Washington commences Life as a Surveyor of Lord Fairfax's Estates — His Duties in that Capacity — First Military Appointment — Accompanies his Brother to Barbadoes — Takes the Small-Pox in the natural Way in that Island — Approach of the Seven Years' War — New Commission as Adjutant-General of the Northern Division.

WE have now reached the period in the life of Washington, when he may be considered as passing from boyhood to youth, and when the serious, though unconscious, training for his great public career began. His older brother Lawrence, who stood to him in many respects in the place of a parent, had removed to the estate near Hunting Creek to which he gave the name of MOUNT VERNON, in honor of his friend the "gallant Vernon," the commander of the naval expedition against the Spanish Main, commemorated in "Thomson's Seasons." George had ever been a favorite with his brother Lawrence, and on leaving school went to reside at Mount Vernon. His time was passed, in the pleasant season of the year, in the usual round of plantation employment, visiting, and sports; and in the winter was devoted to his favorite study of surveying. By way of practice, accurate plans were taken by him of Hunting Creek and the neighboring estates, some of which are still preserved among his papers.

His brother Lawrence had lately married the daughter of Mr. William Fairfax, the proprietor of the neighboring property of Belvoir and the near relative of Lord Fairfax, who was at that time his guest at that plantation. Lord Fairfax was the owner of immense domains in

Virginia. He had inherited through his mother, the daughter of Lord Culpepper the original grantee, a vast tract of land, originally including the entire territory between the Potomac and Rappahannoc rivers. The grant was probably intended to be bounded on the west by the Blue Ridge. But the geography of the interior of the American continent was but little known ; grants were made in the early charters of all the lands lying between certain rivers, (supposed in all cases to run due east and west from the mountains to the sea,) or between certain parallels of latitude from ocean to ocean. The land-agents of Lord Fairfax were not slow in making the discovery, that the upper waters of the Potomac penetrated the Blue Ridge, and that consequently his Lordship's possessions might be construed to extend far into the valley of the Shenandoah. By way of confirming his claim to these extensive territories, he left the residence of his kinsman at Belvoir, built a substantial stone-house in the valley, called Greenway Court, and there established himself in a kind of baronial state in the wilderness.

Lord Fairfax was a man of cultivated mind, educated at Oxford, the associate of the wits of London, the author of one or two papers in the "Spectator,"* and an *habitué* of the polite circles of the metropolis. A disappointment in love is said to have cast a shadow over his after-life, and to have led him to pass his time in voluntary exile on his Virginia estates, watching and promoting the rapid devel-

* In Chalmers's *Biographical Dictionary* we read: "The biographer of Lord Fairfax informs us he was one of the writers of the *Spectator*, but the annotators on that work have not been able to ascertain any of his papers." He may have been the author of some of the anonymous communications sent to the "Letter-box," to which Steele often had recourse in making up a number.

opment of the resources of the country, following the hounds through the primeval wilderness, and cheering his solitary hours by reading and a limited society of chosen friends. George Washington had early attracted his notice as a frequent visitor at Belvoir.

About the time that George came to reside at Mount Vernon, George William Fairfax, the son of the proprietor of Belvoir, had married the daughter of Colonel Carey, of Hampton, on James River, and had brought home his bride and her sister to his father's house. Washington's boyish manuscripts betray the secret of a youthful but not successful passion for a person, whom he does not name, but whom he describes in prose and verse as a "lowland beauty," and whom tradition represents as Miss Grimes, who afterwards married a Colonel Lee and became the mother of General Harry Lee of the

Revolutionary war, at all times a favorite of Washington, perhaps on the mother's account. The confidential letters of Washington to his young friends represent him as finding solace at Belvoir, in the society of the bride's sister, for the still lingering regrets of his boyish " lowland " disappointment.

But his residence at Mount Vernon and his visits at Belvoir were productive of much more important results, and formed a very important link in the chain of events, which decided his fortunes for life. The vast possessions of Lord Fairfax were as yet unsurveyed, and " squatters " (as settlers without title are called in the United States) were beginning to seat themselves on the best of his lands. There was at this period no general system of public surveys executed by authority, and the individual proprietor, after obtaining his grant, was obliged to procure the survey of his lands, by licensed surveyors, on his own responsibility. Lord Fairfax had formed so favorable an opinion of young Washington, that he determined to employ him on the important service of surveying his extensive estates; and he set off on his first expedition just a month from the time he had completed his sixteenth year, accompanied by young Fairfax, the son of the proprietor of Belvoir.

The best idea of the nature of the service in which he was now engaged, will be formed from an extract from one of his own letters:—"Your letter," says he to his correspondent, "gave me the more pleasure, as I received it among barbarians and an uncouth set of people. Since you received my letter of October last, I have not slept above three or four nights in a bed; but after walking a good deal all the day, I have lain down before the fire upon a little hay, straw, fodder, or a bear-skin, — whichsoever was to be had, — with man, wife, and children, like dogs and cats; and happy is he who gets the berth nearest the fire. Nothing would make it pass off tolerably but a good reward. A doubloon is my constant gain every day that the weather will permit my going out, and sometimes six pistoles. The coldness of the weather will not allow of my making a long stay, as the lodging is rather too cold for the time of year. I have never had my clothes off, but have lain and slept in them, except the few nights I have been in Fredericksburg."

The hardships of this occupation will not be fully comprehended by those who are acquainted with the surveyor's duties, only as they are practised in old and thickly settled countries. In addition to the want of accommodation, and the other privations alluded to in the letter just cited, the service was attended with serious peril. In new countries of which "squatters" have begun to take possession, the surveyor is at all times a highly unwelcome visitant, and sometimes goes about his duty at the risk of his life. Besides this, a portion of the country traversed by Washington formed a part of that debatable land, the disputed right to which was the original moving cause of the Seven Years' war. The French were already in motion, both from Canada and Louisiana, to preoccupy the banks of the Ohio, and the savages in their interest roamed the intervening country up to the settlements of Virginia.

Washington was employed in the survey of Lord Fairfax's lands for three years, passing the pleasant season in the wilderness, and spending his winters at Fredericksburg and Mount Vernon. The

out-door, active life fortified his health
and strengthened his frame. His surveys
were executed in part in the very region
which became the theatre of his campaigns in the Seven Years' war. While
engaged in the field he saw something
of life and manners among the friendly
Indians. He probably availed himself of
opportunities to inspect valuable tracts of
ungranted land, which afterwards turned
to good account. At a time when the
minds of men were but little awakened
to the future of the then unsettled West,
he learned from actual observation to
appreciate its vast importance. He soon
became distinguished for the accuracy of
his surveys, and obtained the appointment of a public surveyor, which enabled him to enter his plans as legally
valid, in the county offices. The imperfect manner in which land-surveys at
that time were generally executed, led in

the sequel to constant litigation; but an experienced practitioner in the Western courts pronounced, in after-years, that of all the surveys which had come within his knowledge, those of Washington could alone be depended upon.*

His experience in border life prepared him for his military education, which was now about to commence. No military schools existed at that time even in the mother-country; as late as the last generation, the Duke of Wellington was sent to a military school at Angers, in France, for want of institutions of that kind at home. The restlessness of the French and Indians, on the frontier, to which allusion has just been made, had as early as 1751 begun to create uneasiness in several of the Anglo-American colonies. The Assembly of Virginia divided that province into several military commands

* *Everett's Orations*, vol. iii. p. 440.

or districts, and in one of them Washington, now nineteen years of age, received the appointment of adjutant-general, with the rank of major. His duty was to assemble and exercise the militia, inspect their arms, and train them for actual service in the event of a rupture. In connection with these duties, he gave his time and thoughts to his own preparation for the field. He read military treatises, acquainted himself with the manual exercise, and through the instructions of his brother and other officers of the late war whom he met at Mount Vernon, became expert in the use of the sword.

In these occupations he was interrupted by a painful domestic occurrence. His brother Lawrence, naturally of a feeble constitution, had suffered in his health from the effects of the campaign on the Spanish Main. He became consumptive and was ordered to the West Indies.

George was selected to accompany him. They sailed for Barbadoes in September, 1751, and arrived after a five weeks' voyage. Experiencing no permanent relief in that island, the invalid determined to remove to Bermuda in the spring, and George was sent back to Virginia, to conduct the wife of Lawrence to the last-named island. He arrived in February, after a most tempestuous voyage; but the rapidly declining health of his brother caused the other portion of the arrangement just mentioned to be abandoned. While in Barbadoes in the autumn of 1751, George took the small-pox in the natural way. He had it severely, but owing to the mildness of the climate, the strength of his constitution, and good medical aid, he recovered in three weeks. He was, however, slightly marked through life. His journals kept at Barbadoes evince the spirit of accurate observation which was so prominent a feature of his character. The very first campaign of the Revolutionary war gave proof, that his having had the small-pox in his youth was one of the providential events of his life. That loathsome disease, not yet robbed of its terrors by vaccination, made its appearance in the besieging army before Boston, but the life of its commander was safe.

His brother Lawrence returned home in the summer of 1752; he had derived no material improvement from his voyage, and died in a short time at the age of thirty-four, leaving a large fortune to an infant daughter. George was appointed one of the executors of his will, by which, in the event of the daughter's decease, Mount Vernon was bequeathed to him. Although the youngest of the executors, in consequence of his more thorough knowledge of his brother's affairs the responsible management of his extensive estates devolved upon him. He did not, however, allow these private engagements to interfere with his public duties. As the probability of a collision on the frontier increased, greater attention was paid to the military organization of the province. On the arrival of Governor Dinwiddie in 1752, it was divided into four military districts; and Washington's appointment was renewed as adjutant-general of the northern division, in which several counties were included. The duties devolving upon him, under this new commission, in attending the reviews of the militia and superintending their exercises, were performed with a punctuality and zeal, which rapidly drew toward him the notice and favor of the community.

CHAPTER III.

Commencement of Settlements in the West — The Ohio Company — Hostile Movements of the French — Washington's Perilous Expedition to Venango — Disastrous Campaign of 1754 — Braddock's Expedition and Defeat in 1755 — Arduous and Responsible Duties of Washington during the War — Expedition against Fort Duquesne — And its Capture.

WE now approach the commencement of Washington's public career, and of a train of events of great magnitude and interest; — a service which, though on a small scale and performed at the age of twenty-one, developed much of the mature strength of his character. The struggle of France and England for the exclusive possession of the Eastern portion of the American continent, (for the vast region lying West of the Mississippi

was as yet unknown to both,) was a
principal cause of the European wars of
the last century. England had established
her prosperous colonies along the Atlantic
coast. France had intrenched herself at
the mouth of the St. Lawrence and the
Mississippi, and aimed, by a chain of
posts drawn North and South through
the interior, to prevent the progress of
the English colonists Westward, and con-
fine them within constantly reduced limits; hoping, no doubt, ultimately to drive
them from the continent. This struggle
postponed the civilization of America for
a hundred years. It was the great national drama of the eighteenth century.
In its progress, it subjected the entire
frontier to all the horrors of a remorse-
less border and savage war; and it resulted in the expulsion of the French
from the North American continent; in
reducing the British dominions to a por-

tion of the territory (the Canadian provinces) which had been wrested from France, and in the establishment of the Independence of the United States of America. Everything which preceded the treaty of peace at Aix-la-Chapelle in 1748, may be considered as preliminary to the grand series of events on which we now enter, and in which Washington is immediately to perform a conspicuous, and eventually, the most important part.

Up to this time, the fertile region West of the Alleghany Mountains, and now containing nearly half of the population of the United States, was, with the exception of a few scattered French trading posts and missionary stations, unoccupied by civilized man. In the Western part of the State of Maine, in the entire State of Vermont, and in the Western portions of New York, Pennsylvania, and Virginia, in Kentucky and the States

South of it in the rear of the Carolinas and Georgia, in the entire territory Northwest of the Ohio, and West of the Mississippi,— a region now inhabited by fifteen millions of people,— there did not, in the middle of the last century, arise the smoke of a single hamlet inhabited by the 'descendants of Englishmen. On the return of peace between France and England in 1748, the Ohio Company was formed. Its object was the occupation and settlement of the fertile country Southeast of the Ohio and West of the Alleghany Mountains. It consisted of a small number of gentlemen in Virginia and Maryland, with one associate in London, Mr. Thomas Hanbury, a distinguished merchant of that city. Lawrence Washington was largely interested and actively engaged in the enterprise. A grant of five hundred thousand acres of land was obtained of the crown, by the terms of

which the company were obliged to intro-
duce a hundred families into the territory
within seven years, and to build a fort
and furnish a garrison adequate for their
defence. Out of this germ of private enterprise grew the Seven Years' war, and
by no doubtful chain of cause and effect,
the war of American Independence.

The Ohio Company proceeded to fulfil
the conditions of their grant. Preparations for Indian trade were made; a road
across the mountains, substantially on the
line of that constructed in after-years by
federal authority, was laid out; and an
agent sent to conciliate the Indian tribes.
In 1752 a treaty was entered into between commissioners of Virginia and the
Indians, by which the latter agreed not
to molest any settlements which might
be formed by the company on the South-
eastern side of the Ohio. On the faith
of this compact, twelve families of ad-

venturers from Virginia, headed by Captain Gist, proceeded to establish themselves on the banks of the Monongahela.

These movements were viewed with jealousy by the French colonial government in Canada. Although Great Britain and France had recently concluded a treaty of peace, emissaries were sent from Canada to induce the Indians ou the Ohio to break up the friendly agreement just entered into with Virginia. Some of the traders, it was said, were seized and sent to France; and by orders of the French government a fort was immediately commenced on a branch of French Creek, about fifteen miles South of Lake Erie, as a position from which the Indians could be controlled and the Virginians held in check. These proceedings were promptly reported to Governor Dinwiddie by the servants of the Ohio Company, and the governor immediately determined to make them the subject of remonstrance addressed to the French commandant; rather, it may be supposed, with a view to ascertain precisely the facts of the case by a special messenger, than on a supposition that movements of this kind could be arrested by anything less than the interference of the supreme authority at Paris and London.

It was no easy matter to transmit an official message, in the state of the country at that time, from the banks of James River to the shores of Lake Erie. The distance to be travelled was between five and six hundred miles, the greater part of the way through a wilderness. Mountains were to be climbed and rivers crossed; tribes of savages occupied a considerable portion of the intervening space, and all the hazards of an Indian frontier, in a state of daily increasing irritation, were to be encountered. To all these difficulties, the season of the year (it was now November) added obstacles all but insuperable, in the absence of artificial communications. It is not to be wondered at, that some persons to whom Governor Dinwiddie first proposed the service should excuse themselves. It was offered to Major Washington and by him promptly accepted, although the decease of his brother had thrown upon him domestic duties, which would have furnished an honest excuse for shrinking from the laborious and dangerous commission. But Washington never shrunk from the performance of a duty. He received his instructions, and started from Williamsburg on the 30th of November, 1753.

He was joined at Captain Gist's settlement on the Monongahela by that brave pioneer of civilization. At Logstown he held a conference with Tanacharison, who was the chief or half-king of the friendly Indians seated there, and who, with two or three others of the natives, accompanied Washington and Gist first to Venango, — a post on the French Creek, — and then to the head-quarters of M. de St. Pierre, the French commandant, a short distance farther to the North. Here Washington performed his errand, by delivering his despatches and receiving the reply of the commandant; carefully noting the character and strength of the place, and gaining such information as he was able of the extent of the military operations in progress. The return journey was a series of the severest exposures and the most imminent perils. Their wearied horses were sent by land back to Venango; while Washington and his associates in a canoe descended the river, swollen by wintry rains and at best of hazardous navigation. At Venango, they had reason to suspect hostile

intentions from the French and savages,
and Washington and Gist, with a single
Indian guide, in order to hasten their
return to the settlements, started through
the wilderness on foot, with their packs
on their shoulders and guns in their
hands. They were dogged through the
woods by Indians in the French interest.
Their guide exerted all the arts of savage
cunning, after leading them out of their
path in the forest, to get possession of
Washington's gun, but without success.
Baffled by their wariness, and perceiving
them at nightfall to be fatigued by the
weary march, he turned upon them, and
at a distance of fifteen feet fired with his
double-barrelled rifle; but without injur-
ing either of them. Gist would have put
him to death on the spot, but Washington
insisted upon sparing his life, justly as it
had been forfeited. After detaining him
to a late hour, they allowed him to es-

cape, and in order to forestall an attack, from such confederates as he might have lurking in the woods, they pursued their own journey, weary as they were, through the long December's night.

Not doubting that the savages would soon be on their trail, they dared not stop till they reached the Alleghany River, a clear and rapid stream, which they hoped to be able to cross on the ice, — their only consolation under the stinging severity of the weather. The river unfortunately was neither frozen across nor wholly open; but fringed with ice for fifty yards on each shore, and the middle stream filled with cakes of ice furiously drifting down the current. With "one poor hatchet," to use Washington's own expression, they commenced the con-struction of a raft, which it took them all day to complete. They launched it upon the river, but were soon so surrounded and wedged in by drifting masses of ice, that they expected every. moment that their raft would go to pieces, and they themselves be hurled into the water, at the extreme peril of their lives. Washington put out his pole to stop the raft, till the fields of ice should float by ; but the raft was urged with so much violence upon his pole, that he himself, holding to it, was thrown into the river, where it was ten feet deep. He saved his life by clinging to a log ; but unable to force the raft to either shore, they were compelled to leave it, and passed the night on an island in the middle of the river. So intense was the cold, that the hands and feet of Captain Gist, an experienced woodsman, were frozen. Happily the river froze wholly over during the night, and they were enabled to cross to the opposite bank in the morning on the ice. To this circumstance they were indebted no doubt for their escape from the tomahawk of the pursuing savages.

The foregoing adventure has been given in some detail from Washington's official report, which was sent by Governor Dinwiddie to London and there published. It throws light on traits of his character, which in after-life have been somewhat overlooked, in consequence of the habitual circumspection and prudence which were forced upon him by circumstances, during his revolutionary career. This dangerous errand was undertaken by Washington through an unsettled wilderness, infested by savages, at a season of the year when the huntsman in his log cabin shrinks from the storm; and this not by a penniless adventurer, taking desperate risks for promotion and bread; but by a young man allied by blood and connected by friendship with the most influential families in the colony, possessed of property

in his own right, with large presump-
tive expectations. In this his first official
service, undertaken under these circumstances, he displayed the courage, the
presence of mind, the fortitude, the endurance, the humanity (on a small scale
indeed, but at the risk of his life, in pre-
serving that of the treacherous savage),
which, throughout his career, never failed
to mark his conduct.

Although war was not formally declared
between France and England till May,
1756, hostilities broke out the following
year (1754) along the frontier of the
Anglo-American colonies. Preparations, of
which the promise was greater than the
reality, were made by the provincial assemblies and governors. The Ohio Company commenced a fort at the confluence
of the Monongahela and the Alleghany,
and a regiment, feeble in numbers, "self-
willed and ungovernable," of which Wash-

ington was second in command, was sent to their support. The movements of the French were more prompt and formidable; a large force of Europeans and savages in their interest came down from Venango, the servants of the Ohio Land Company were captured or driven from the work which they had commenced at the junction of the rivers, and Fort Duquesne was erected on the spot. This was the first blow struck in the great Seven Years' War; and it is a memorable incident in the life of Washington, then but twenty-two years of age, and accidentally in command of a trifling force in the unsettled region beyond the Alleghanies, that it devolved on him to repel it.

He immediately sent despatches to the neighboring governors requesting aid; but without waiting for the greatly needed reinforcements, pushed on through the wilderness to the defence of the frontier. Receiving intelligence from the friendly Indians that a party of the enemy was lurking in the woods, Washington, ignorant of their strength and in order to be prepared for an emergency, threw up a slight .work at a place called the "Great Meadows," and which he described as "a charming field for an encounter." Having here received more particular information from Captain Gist and the friendly Indians of the whereabout of the enemy, he came upon them by surprise, after a forced march by night, with a company of picked men. In the conflict that ensued, ten of the French, including their leader Jumonville, were killed, and twenty-one made prisoners.

By the death of Colonel Fry at Will's Creek, on the way to join the little army, Washington became its Commander-in-chief. Reinforcements were put in motion; but none arrived, with the exception of an independent company from South Carolina, about a hundred strong, who reached the Great Meadows under Captain Mackay. The main body of the French at Fort Duquesne, with their Indian allies, were believed greatly to outnumber the Anglo-Americans. Aware that as soon as the fate of Jumonville should become known to the French commandant a formidable force would be sent against him, Washington strengthened his position at the Great Meadows, by an intrenchment and palisade, and called the work "Fort Necessity." Burdened by the Indians, who crowded his camp with their families, and harassed by the claims of precedence on the part of Captain Mackay, he made an advance movement, by a very laborious march, with a large portion of his force, to the Monongahela. So difficult was the coun-

try for artillery, that ten days were required for a distance of thirteen miles.
Arrived at Gist's Settlement, he received
intelligence from deserters and Indians,
that Fort Duquesne had been strongly
reinforced by troops from Canada, and
savages under the French influence. Ap-
prehending an attack, he ordered up Captain Mackay, who had been left with the
reserve at the Great Meadows, to his
support, who promptly obeyed the sum-
mons. It was decided, however, by a
council of war, that it would be unsafe
to risk a battle in the open field, and a
retreat to Fort Necessity was determined
on. This was effected with difficulty in
two days; and as the troops from fatigue
and want of provisions were unable to
pursue the march, it was concluded to
make a stand, and await the enemy
within their intrenchments.

The fort was soon invested by the

French and Indians, who were able on one point to command the interior of the work. A severe action commenced on the 3d of July, and was prolonged till late in the evening. A capitulation was then proposed by the French commander and accepted by Washington. It was drawn up in a drenching rain at night, after a hard-fought day, in the French language, and signed by Washington, not knowing that through the fraud or ignorance of his interpreter, Van Braam, the death of Jumonville was called, in the act of capitulation, an "assassination," — a circumstance which was made a futile subject of reproach to Washington in France at the time, and has been occasionally revived since. The following day, the Fourth of July, he led out his little force from the stockade, and conducted them in safety through ill-restrained bands of savages to Fort Cumberland.

The following year serious efforts were made, both by France and England, to strengthen themselves on the banks of the Ohio. Two regiments were sent from England, under the brave but self-sufficient, obstinate, and unfortunate Braddock. New orders came with them relative to precedence, which disgusted the provincial officers. Washington threw up his commission, but, strongly attached to the profession of arms, he gladly accepted an invitation from General Braddock, to join his military family as a volunteer. Great delays attended the collecting of supplies and forwarding of troops. Washington fell dangerously ill, and was of necessity left behind, determined however to rejoin the army at the first moment of convalescence. The General, inexperienced in the warfare of the wilderness, neglected the measures necessary to conciliate the Indians and the precautions requisite to prevent surprise. Washington arrived at camp but the day before the catastrophe. He was accustomed in after-life to describe the appearance of the army, as they crossed the Monongahela on the 9th of July, and moved forward in confident expectation of reducing Fort Duquesne the following day, as the most magnificent spectacle he had ever beheld. A few hours only passed, before they fell into an ambuscade; the forest rang with the war-whoop of the Indians; the advance under Colonel Gage (afterwards the last royal governor of Massachusetts) was driven back on the main body, which was thereby thrown into confusion; officers and men dropped on every side, under the murderous fire of the enemy, concealed in the woody ravines right and left; and at length the whole force, panic-struck and disorganized, after a terrific and deadly struggle of three hours, in which the loss of the enemy was trifling, suffered a total defeat. "They ran before the French and Indians," says Washington, "like sheep before dogs." Of fourteen hundred and sixty in Braddock's army, officers and privates, four hundred and fifty-six were killed outright, and four hundred and twenty-one were wounded; a greater proportion of killed and wounded than is reported in any of the celebrated actions of the present day. The General himself was mortally wounded, and brought off with difficulty from the field.

Washington acted as the General's aid throughout the engagement; and after the other aids, Orme and Morris, were disabled, the perilous duty devolved exclusively on him. It was performed by him, according to his brother officer Orme, who witnessed his conduct, "with the greatest courage and resolution." "By the all-powerful dispensations of Providence," he writes to his brother, "I have been protected beyond all human probability or expectation; for I had four bullets through my coat, and two horses shot under me; yet I escaped unhurt, though death was levelling my companions on every side." His friend and physician, Dr. Craik, said, "I expected every moment to see him fall." A very curious anecdote has also been preserved, on the authority of Dr. Craik, who relates that when Washington, fifteen years later, made a journey to the Great Kenhawa, he was approached by the chief of a band of Indians, who said that he had come a long distance to see Washington, at whom he had aimed his rifle many times in the battle of the Monongahela, but without effect. —A seal of Washington with his initials, probably shot away from his person, was found, after a lapse of eighty years, on

the field of battle, and is now in the possession of a member of the family.— So
prevalent was the impression of his almost miraculous escape from the perils
of this disastrous day, that President
Davies of New Jersey College, but at
that time a clergyman in Virginia, in a
sermon preached in the month of August
following, before a company of volunteers,
after commending the patriotic ardor which
had been manifested in the colony, added,
"As a remarkable instance of this, I may
point out to the public that heroic youth,
Colonel Washington, whom I cannot but
hope Providence has hitherto preserved
in so signal a manner, for some important
service to his country."

There is certainly something extraordinary in the brilliant reputation with
which Washington, a young officer holding no higher position in the army than
that of a volunteer aid to its unfortunate

chief, returned from this disastrous campaign. His preservation, as we have just seen, was ascribed to nothing less than Providential interposition. The exposed state of the frontier, thrown open to the enemy, required immediate measures of protection. A provincial force of two thousand men was immediately voted by the Assembly, and though the governor was supposed to favor another candidate, the command was given by him to Washington. He received this appointment in four weeks after his return from the battle of the Monongahela. He immediately established his head-quarters at Winchester, then one of the most advanced settlements, and from that point superintended the operations of the Virginia frontier, for the rest of the war. These, with the exception to be presently mentioned, were of a defensive character. No important expeditions were attempted; no great battles fought; but a line of feeble settlements, extending for several hundred miles, was to be protected from roving bands of savages, countenanced by the French commandant, emboldened by the events of 1755, and stimulated to plunder and bloodshed by outcasts from the colonies.

The task of the youthful Commander-in-chief — responsible for the peace of the frontier, but with very inadequate means at his command — was arduous in the extreme. A reluctant and undisciplined militia was to be retained in the ranks by personal influence, — without pay, without clothes, and very imperfectly armed. Contradictory and impracticable orders were continually received from Governor Dinwiddie, who was wholly unskilled in military matters, but obstinately insisted on directing everything. Greedy and dishonest contractors played their ancient game of fraud. The arrogant pretensions of a subaltern officer, bearing a royal commission, kept Fort Cumberland in an unsettled state, and compelled Colonel Washington in midwinter to go to Boston for a solution of the difficulty by Governor Shirley, then the Commander-in-chief of the royal forces on the continent. Wholesale desertions on the approach of danger weakened his little force; and the intrigues of rivals aspiring to his place, and seeking to gain it by traducing his character, outraged his feelings. In his official correspondence for 1756 and 1757, all these sources of embarrassment and annoyance are set forth; and we are struck with the similarity of the state of things then existing, with that to which we shall presently have occasion to advert in the Revolutionary War. While nothing can be conceived more harassing, it must be admitted that it formed the best imaginable school of preparation for the more momentous scenes in which he was hereafter to act a leading part. It was not, however, unattended with personal danger. The fatigues and anxieties which he underwent, again brought on a severe illness, with which he suffered for four months at the close of 1757 and the beginning of 1758.

The campaign of 1758 was devoted to an important military expedition from Pennsylvania and Virginia against Fort Duquesne, in which Washington, as commander of the Virginia contingent, took a leading part. The whole force destined for the expedition was placed under the command of General Forbes; and in consequence of his illness at Philadelphia, the loss of time in opening a new road into the wilderness (contrary to the advice of Washington), and the usual tardiness of military operations in colonies remote · from the seat of power, it was late in the autumn before the army took the field. Washington, at his earnest solicitation, led the advance to scour the forest and open the roads. It was, however, far in November before they reached the neighborhood of Fort Duquesne; and the commander, after a serious check, was on the point of abandoning the enterprise for that year. The report brought by deserters of the weakness of the garrison, determined him, at the last moment, to make the advance; and on the 25th of November, 1758, he arrived at the fort, and found that it had been abandoned and burned by the enemy. The English and provincials erected a temporary work on the spot, to which, in honor of the great minister, who had infused his spirit into the conduct of the war, they gave the name of Fort Pitt, still preserved in that of Pittsburg. The power of France was thus finally subverted on the Ohio, and the Anglo-Saxon race forever established on " the beautiful River." The fall of Quebec the following year, and the provisions of the treaty of 1763, extinguished the French dominion in North America.

CHAPTER IV.

Retirement from the Army — Marriage — Election to the House of Burgesses and Character as a Member — His Occupations as a Planter, and business Habits — Visits the unsettled Parts of the State — Commencement of the Controversy with the Mother-Country — Mistaken Impression that Washington was ever lukewarm in the American Cause — Proofs of the Contrary — His early Career admirably calculated to fit him for the great Work of his life.

THE health of Washington, as we have seen, had suffered severely in the progress of the war. He had made repeated attempts to obtain a commission in the royal army; but, although possessing in the highest degree as a military man the confidence of Governor Dinwiddie, General Braddock, and his successors, those attempts were unsuccessful. Commissions were monopolized by younger sons and the favorites of power at home. Thus was the wish of Washington to enter the royal service baffled a second time. By what narrow chances the fate of empires is determined! Having no prospect of advancement in his favorite profession, and having, in the fall of Fort Duquesne, seen the great object of the contest obtained, as far as Virginia, Maryland, and Pennsylvania were concerned, he determined to retire from public life, and devote himself to the care of his property, which had suffered by neglect, and to the duties of a private citizen.

Having in the course of the preceding year paid his addresses successfully to Mrs. Martha Custis, the widow of Colonel John Custis, of Virginia, he was married to that lady on the 6th of January, 1759. There is a constant tradition that three years before he had been a suitor to Mary Phillipse, the sister-in-law of Colonel

Beverley Robinson, of New York, whose guest he was on his journey to and from the Eastern Colonies in 1756. On this occasion, Colonel Morris, his associate in arms at Braddock's defeat, and his companion in the excursion to the East, having lingered in New York after the return of Washington to the army, proved a successful rival, and became the husband of the lady. She was the heiress of a large landed property in the state of New York, and her family adhered to the royal side in the Revolution. This lady is said to have died in England at the age of ninety-four,—having survived. Washington about twenty-five years. One cannot but bestow a passing thought on the question, what might have been the effect on the march of events, if Washington, at the age of twenty-four, and before the controversies between the mother-country and the colonies had commenced, had formed a matrimonial alliance with a family of wealth and influence in New York, which adhered to the royal cause, and left America as loyalists when the war broke out. It is a somewhat curious fact, that Washington's head-quarters, during a part of the campaign of 1776, were established in the stately mansion of the Morrises, on Harlem River.*

His connection with Mrs. Washington was in all respects fortunate. She was the mother of two children by her former marriage; she brought him a large accession of fortune for those days; and by her solid virtues, cheerful disposition, and simple and amiable manners, relieved him from the cares of domestic life, strengthened the attachment of his friends, and adorned the high public stations to which he was successively called. He remained childless; but he adopted her

* Lossing's *Mount Vernon and its Associations*, p. 46.

children as his own, and superintended their education and managed their fortunes with parental care. The daughter died in early life; the son became an Aid to Washington during the Revolutionary War, but died in 1781, leaving three daughters and a son. The youngest daughter, who afterwards married Lawrence Lewis, Esq., and the son, George W. Parke Custis, who died at Arlington, in Virginia, in the year 1857, were adopted by Washington and brought up at Mount Vernon.

Washington, though absent with the army, had been elected to the Virginia House of Burgesses in 1757. After his retirement from the service, he took his seat, and continued a member of that body under repeated reëlections, till the commencement of the Revolutionary War. He was remarkably diligent and punctual in the performance of his duties as a legislator and a representative, but seldom took part in debate properly so called, and never made a long speech. In this respect he resembles two others of the foremost leaders of the American Revolution, Franklin and Jefferson, men who in general intellectual culture and political training had the advantage of Washington, but who like him had never formed themselves to the habit of debate. His recommendation to a nephew, on being chosen a member of the House of Burgesses, may be taken as the indication of his own rule of conduct: "If you have a mind to command the attention of the House, the only advice I will offer is to speak seldom but on important subjects, except such as particularly relate to your constituents; and in the former case make yourself perfectly master of the subject. Never exceed a decent warmth, and submit your sentiments with diffidence. A dictatorial style, though it may carry conviction, is always accompanied with disgust."

Such was the habit of Washington himself; it was the only course consistent with his natural disposition and peculiar balance of mental qualities. There is no doubt that in this, as in some other respects, the possession of more brilliant qualities would have marred the symmetry of his character and lessened his influence. Shining powers of debate, for instance, had he possessed them, would, by the necessity of that talent, have fixed him as a partisan, and consequently have impaired that influence through which he controlled all parties. As it was, no one possessed greater ascendency in all deliberative bodies of which he was a member. On the return to Virginia of the delegates to the first Continental Congress at Philadelphia, Patrick Henry, himself generally regarded as the first of American orators, was asked who was the greatest man in the assembly. His reply was, "If you speak of eloquence, Mr. Rutledge of South Carolina is by far the greatest orator; but if you speak of solid information and sound judgment, Colonel Washington is unquestionably the greatest man on the floor."

Shortly after his marriage, Washington established his permanent home at Mount Vernon, and gave himself up to the usual routine of plantation life, as pursued in those days. Tobacco was then the great staple product of this part of Virginia, and Washington was in the habit of shipping his crop directly to London, to Liverpool, and to Bristol. All supplies of manufactures for clothing, implements of husbandry, and matters of taste and luxury were derived by direct importation from England, usually twice a year.

All the business connected with the cultivation of his estates and the exportation
of his crops, on the one hand, and the
orders for his return supplies, on the other,
were superintended by him in person. His
letters were written and copied, and his
account-books kept by himself in mer-
cantile order, and with extreme neatness and precision. In the course of
these transactions, the minutest details
of domestic economy necessarily received
his attention, down to the most trifling
article of clothing for the children. While
he gave his hours of labor to these humble occupations, he found a much cherished relaxation in the sports of the
field. He was a bold rider, and followed
the fox-hounds, sometimes two or three
times a week, with untiring spirit. It
is related that at the battle of Princeton,
(where, as he told the painter Trumbull,
he was in greater danger than ever be-

fore in the course of his life, being at one time between the fire of both armies,) perceiving a regiment of the enemy in full retreat down the ˙hill, he leaped his favorite roan hunter over a stone-wall which crowned the summit, gave the view halloo, and said to his aids, " A perfect fox-chase !"

In the year 1770, Washington revisited the scenes of his youthful adventure and service. Accompanied by Dr. Craik, who shared with him the hazards of Braddock's field, and a party of friends and servants, he went on horseback to Pittsburg, then in its infancy, and descended the Ohio River from that place to the mouth of the Great Kenhawa in Virginia. — A net of railroads now covers the region through which they rode, and hundreds of steamers ply the waters of the Ohio. — Washington and his party floated down the river in an open boat, exposed to the savages on the right bank, on which at that time there were no white settlements, and obliged to land at night and encamp in the woods. Having reached the Kenhawa, they ascended that stream, and made valuable selections of fertile lands. It was on this occasion that the interview with the Indian chief took place, which has been already described. One object of this excursion was to select and mark out the lands, granted by the colonial government, as a bounty to the soldiers who had served in the war.

The contest of legislation had been for some years in progress, which preluded the great scene of Washington's services and fame, — the American Revolution. With a view to American revenue, the Stamp Act was passed. It was repealed, but with the assertion of a right to tax America; and this theory, carried out in

practice by the enactment of the duties
on tea, glass, and painters' colors, of which
the first-named was persistently retained
when the others were rescinded, brought
on the war.   These ill-advised measures,
which we have grouped in a sentence,
were spread over eight years of irritation,
disaffection, and ripening revolt.   Washington, by nature the most loyal of men
to order and law, whose rule of social
life was obedience to rightful authority,
was from the first firmly on the American side; not courting, not contemplating
even, till the eve of the explosion, a forcible resistance to the mother-country, but
not recoiling from it, when forced upon
the colonies as the inevitable result of
their principles.   An impression has existed in some quarters on the other side
of the Atlantic, that Washington originally
leaned to the royalist side in the great
conflict of opinion and feeling that pre-

ceded the Revolutionary War. His correspondence, not less than his public course as a member of the House of Burgesses, shows this impression to be utterly groundless. It may have had its origin in the fact, that, not being a public speaker or writer, he was less frequently and prominently brought before the public as an open champion of the cause, than some of the other leaders of the Revolution. The spurious letters bearing his name, and which were industriously published in a volume at London during the war, in order to shake the faith of his countrymen in his integrity, contributed no doubt to strengthen this impression. It is matter of surprise that the title of a fabrication of this kind, which one is pleased to think would, at this time of day, be deemed unworthy a place among the instruments of honorable warfare, should be admitted as a genuine publication into respectable literary manuals.*

Washington was the near neighbor and confidential friend of George Mason, who drew the plan of the association not to import British manufactures in 1774; and in the absence of Mason from the House of Burgesses, and as chairman of the meeting at which the resolves were adopted, he presented it to the assembly. There is not the slightest trace of dissent on his part from any of the measures of the popular leaders, except that he deemed it wrong to forbid the export of American produce to England, as this was the only fund out of which the colonies were able to pay their debts to the British manufacturer. His name is found in conjunction with those of the most constant patriots, in the anxious years that preceded the appeal to arms; and

* Lowndes's *Bibliographers' Manual.*

when the House of Burgesses was dissolved by the royal governor in the summer of 1774, Washington was a member of the convention chosen to take its place, and was, with five associates, elected a delegate to the first Continental Congress, which met in Philadelphia in the autumn of that year. Of his position in that assembly, the estimate formed by Patrick Henry, one of the most fervid of patriots, has already been given. A letter written by him from Philadelphia to one of his former companions in arms, Captain Mackenzie, then stationed at Boston, exhibits the state of Washington's mind at this period, as of that of the class of men whom he represented. The following extract will suffice: "I think I can announce it as a fact, that it is not the wish nor the interest of the government of Massachusetts, or any other government upon this continent, separately or

collectively, to set up for independence;
but this you may rely upon, that none
of them will ever submit to the loss
of those valuable rights and privileges,
which are essential to the inhabitants of
every free State, and without which life,
liberty, and property are rendered totally
insecure." The object of holding the congress, — as expressed in the resolution of
the convention of delegates in Virginia,
by which Washington and his associates
were elected, — was declared to be, " to
consider the most proper and effectual
manner of so operating upon the commercial connection of the colonies with
the mother-country, as to procure re-
dress for the much injured province
of Massachusetts Bay, to secure British
America from the ravage and ruin of
arbitrary taxes, and speedily to procure
the return of that harmony and union,
so beneficent to the whole empire, and

so ardently desired by all British America."

The Congress met at Philadelphia on the 5th of September. Washington's letter to Captain Mackenzie was written on the 9th of October, and the petition to the King, which closes the journal of the session, terminates with the following loyal aspirations: "That your Majesty may enjoy every felicity, through a long and glorious reign, over loyal and happy subjects, and that your descendants may inherit your prosperity and your dominions, till time shall be no more, is, and always will be, our sincere and fervent prayer!"

Before we enter upon a brief survey of the career of Washington, as the great military leader of the American Revolution, we cannot but reflect upon the adaptation of the first portion of his life, as a school of preparation for the sequel.

His great vocation may be considered as commencing with the Revolutionary War. He was the providentially appointed leader of that great contest, whose results, direct and remote, are of equal moment to the Old World and the New. We can scarcely imagine a course of life better fitted to train him for his arduous work than that which he led from the age of sixteen, when he entered the wilderness as a surveyor of unsettled lands, to his retirement from the army eleven years afterwards. In this period he had received a thorough athletic training, and had studied the art of war, not on the blackboard at military schools, but in actual service, and that of the most perilous and trying kind, under rigid disciplinarians of the best school of that day; for Braddock had been selected for the command, as an experienced and thoroughly accomplished officer.

But military command was but one part
of the career which awaited Washington. Almost all the duties of government
centred in his hands, under the ineffi-
cient administration of the old congress.
A merely military education would have
furnished no adequate preparation for the
duties to be performed by him. It was
accordingly a most auspicious circumstance that from the year 1759 to the
Revolution he passed fifteen years as a
member of the House of Burgesses, where
he acquired a familiar knowledge of civil
affairs and of politics. The ordinary legislation of a leading colonial government,
like that of Virginia, was no mean school
of political experience; and the state of
affairs at the time was such as to expand and elevate the minds of men.
Everything was inspired with an un-
consciously developed, but not the less
stirring revolutionary energy; and many

of his associates were men of large views and strenuous character.

While his public duties, civil and military, prepared him, in this way, for the positions he was to fill in war and in peace, the fifteen years which he passed in the personal management of a large landed estate, and the care of an ample fortune, furnished abundant occasion for the formation of the economical side of his character, and gave a thoroughness to his administrative habits, which has not been witnessed in the career of many very eminent public men in Europe or America. It will not be easy to find another instance of a great military and political leader, who, to the same degree, has been equal to the formation and execution of the boldest plans, and to the control of the most perplexed combinations of affairs, and yet not above the most ordinary details of business, nor negligent of minute economies. But it was precisely this union of seemingly inconsistent qualities of mind and character, which was most needed from the time he took command of the Revolutionary Army to the close of his Presidential service.

CHAPTER V.

Commencement of the War — Lexington and Concord —
The Royal Army blockaded in Boston — Washington
chosen Commander-in-Chief by the Continental Congress — Destitute Condition of the Army — Dorchester
Heights fortified in the Spring of 1776 — Boston evacuated by the Royal Forces — The War transferred to
New York — Disastrous Battle of Long Island — Washington Retreats through New Jersey to Philadelphia —
Recrosses the Delaware and surprises the Hessians at
Trenton — Gains the Battle of Princeton and retrieves
the Fortune of the Campaign.

To do full justice to the character of
Washington, as the great leader of the
American Revolution, would require a detailed history of the war, by which the
Independence of the United States was
established, and, of consequence, greatly
exceed the limits of this work. A very
brief sketch of those events in which he
was directly concerned, is all that can be
attempted.

It may first be observed, that it would be unjust to Washington to place his military reputation on ordinary strategical grounds. He had an army to call into being, as well as to conduct; the entire *matériel* of war to create; supplies to raise, without credit or the power of taxation, from a small and scattered population, subject to separate state governments, and not yet organized under one efficient central authority. At no period of the war was he supported by a strong civil power, for Congress acted only by recommendations addressed to the states; he was never furnished with a well-supplied military chest, (there was a moment in the disastrous campaign of 1776, when he wrote to Mr. Morris at Philadelphia, that a hundred pounds would be of great service to him,) and he never was at the head of what, at the present day, would be called an efficient force; unless we except the allied American and French army at Yorktown, and there he achieved a brilliant success. It would of course be unreasonable, under these circumstances, to compare his military operations with those of the great captains of Europe, who, in the service of rich and powerful governments, and at the head of immense bodies of veteran troops, with the aid of experienced subalterns in every rank of the army, and with a boundless supply of all the *matériel* of war, gain the victories which fill the pages of history and earn for themselves immortal fame.

The actual commencement of hostilities in the war of the American Revolution might be said to be accidental. A series of ill-judged and oppressive measures on the part of the British Parliament, aimed principally at the province of Massachusetts Bay (as it was then called), had produced a great degree of irritation there, in which the other colonies cordially sympathized. Military preparations had been going on for a year or two in Massachusetts, and small stores of powder and arms had been collected. A few field-pieces had been procured at Concord, a village lying about eighteen miles west of Boston; and this fact coming to the knowledge of General Gage, the royal governor and commander-in-chief in Boston, he despatched a considerable force into the country, on the night of the 18th of April, 1775, with the twofold object of destroying the provincial stores, and, as was supposed, of arresting Hancock and Adams, who had been proscribed by name, and who were then at Lexington, a village situated on the road to Concord. This rash movement brought on a collision at Lexington and Concord on the morning of the 19th, between the

royal force and the militia of those
places and others on the line of march
and in the vicinity; blood was shed on
both sides; the alarm spread with great
rapidity through the neighboring towns;
and the royal force was saved from an-
nihilation, only by a disorderly and tu-
multuous retreat to Boston. Here they
were immediately blockaded by fifteen or
twenty thousand men of the militia of
Massachusetts and the other New England colonies, who, as the news of
the commencement of hostilities spread
through the country, had poured in from
every side. As Massachusetts was the
seat of the war, the control of this force
and the conduct of the struggle, thus
improvised, devolved, by the necessity of
the case, and by tacit understanding, upon
the Provincial Congress (as it was called)
of that colony,— an extra-constitutional
body called into existence by the exi-

gency of the times, and assimilated as nearly as possible to the Assembly organized under the Colonial Charter. Major-General Ward, of Massachusetts, thus became, by acquiescence, the commander-in-chief of the forces hastily assembled around Boston. The second session of the Continental Congress commenced at Philadelphia about three weeks after the events at Lexington and Concord, and measures were immediately adopted for recognizing the forces already concentrated round Boston, as a Continental Army, and for raising additional troops in the other states.

Early in June, 1775, the question of the appointment of a commander-in-chief came up. Colonel Washington, as has been seen, was one of the delegates from Virginia to the Continental Congress. His distinguished services in the Seven Years' War were still freshly remembered; and

he had acquired in the intervening period, in the Virginia Assembly, a substantial reputation for prudence, energy, and
practical wisdom. Combined with this
reputation, his large fortune, his attrac-
tive and imposing personal appearance
and manners, and general weight of character, gave him influence; and motives of
patriotic expediency inclined the delegates from Massachusetts, and especially
their ardent and eloquent leader, John
Adams, afterwards the second President
of the United States, to waive whatever
claim that colony might be supposed to
possess, and to give their support to the
accomplished Virginia colonel, as Commander-in-chief of the Continental Armies.
Washington was unanimously elected; and
in accepting the appointment, which he
did in person in his place in Congress,
he modestly avowed his " consciousness
that his abilities and military experience

might not be equal to the extensive and important trust;" and added, "lest some unlucky event should happen unfavorable to my reputation, I beg it may be remembered by every gentleman in the room, that I this day declare, with the utmost sincerity, that I do not think myself equal to the command I am honored with." The compensation of the Commander-in-chief having, before the election, been fixed at five hundred dollars per month, he declined to accept any salary; but stated that he should keep an exact account of his expenses, not doubting that these would be reimbursed to him by Congress. This account is in existence, wholly made out in Washington's handwriting. It has been lithographed in fac-simile, and is a document of great curiosity and interest. Washington's commission passed Congress on the 17th of June, 1775, the day on which the memorable battle of Bunker Hill was fought. The news of that battle reached him on his way to join the army before Boston ; and on learning that the militia had sustained themselves gallantly in a conflict with regular troops, he declared that the cause of America was safe.

He arrived in Cambridge, Massachusetts, on the 2d of July, and on the following day presented himself at the head of the army. His head-quarters remained at Cambridge,* till the evacuation of Boston by the royal forces on the 17th of March, 1776. The position of affairs was one of vast responsibility and peril. The country at large was highly excited, and expected that a bold stroke would be struck and decisive successes obtained. But the army was without organization

---

* Washington's head-quarters at Cambridge were established in the house now owned and occupied by Mr. Longfellow, then belonging to the loyalist family of Vassall.

and discipline; the troops unused to obey, the officers for the most part unaccustomed, some of them incompetent, to command. A few of them only had had a limited experience in the Seven Years' War. Most of the men had rushed to the field on the first alarm of hostilities, without any enlistment; and when they were enlisted, it was only till the end of the year. There was no military chest; scarce anything that could be called a commissariat. The artillery consisted of a few old field-pieces of various sizes, served with a very few exceptions by persons wholly untrained in gunnery. There was no siege train, and an almost total want of every description of ordnance stores. Barrels of sand, represented as powder, were from time to time brought into the camp, to prevent the American army itself from being aware of its deficiency in that respect. In the autumn of 1775, an alarm of small-pox was brought from Boston, and the troops were subjected to inoculation. There was no efficient power, either in the Provincial Assembly or the Congress at Philadelphia, by which these wants could be supplied and these evils remedied. Such were the circumstances under which General Washington took the field, at the head of a force greatly superior in numbers to the royal army, but in all other respects a very unequal match. Meantime the British were undisputed masters of the approaches to Boston by water.

Washington's letters disclose extreme impatience under the inaction to which he was condemned; but the gravest difficulties attended the expulsion of the royal forces from Boston. It could only be effected by the bombardment and assault of that place; an attempt which must in any event have been destruc-

tive to the large non-combatant population, that had been unable to remove
into the country, and which would have
been of doubtful success, for the want of
a siege train, and with troops wholly
unused to such an undertaking. Having in the course of the year received
some captured ordnance from Canada,
and a supply of ammunition taken
by privateers at sea, Washington was
strongly disposed to assault the town, as
soon as the freezing of the bay on the
western side of the peninsula would allow the troops to pass on the ice. The
winter, however, remained open longer
than usual, and a council of war dis-
suaded this attempt. He then determined
to occupy Nook's Hill, (an eminence at
the extremity of Dorchester "Neck," as
it was called, separated from Boston by
a narrow arm of the harbor,) and Dorchester Heights, which commanded Nook's

Hill and the town itself. In this way the royal forces would be compelled to take the risk of a general action, for the purpose of dislodging the Americans, or else to evacuate the town. The requisite preparations having been made with secrecy, energy, and despatch, the heights were covered with breastworks on the night of the 4th of March, 1776, as " by enchantment." A partial movement, undertaken by the royal army to dislodge the Americans, was frustrated by stress of weather; and on the 17th of March, in virtue of an agreement to that effect with the municipal government, the town and harbor of Boston were evacuated by the British army and navy without firing a gun. Thus, without a battle and without the destruction of a building in Boston, the first year of the war was brought to a successful and an auspicious close.

The British army under General Howe,

after evacuating Boston, sailed for Halifax; but in the course of the summer a general concentration of the royal forces took place in the vicinity of New York, Staten Island being the head-quarters. There the landing of the British was effected, on the same day on which the Independence of the United States was declared at Philadelphia. General Howe was reinforced at Staten Island by the troops under Clinton and Cornwallis, who had been despatched to the South, and who had been repulsed in an attack upon Sullivan's Island, which was defended with signal valor and success by General Moultrie. A naval armament, with a large reinforcement of German mercenaries, also arrived at New York under Lord Howe, (the brother of the general,) who was clothed with powers as a commissioner, and who brought unavailing overtures for pacification. These he addressed, at first, to "George Washington, *Esq.;*" afterwards, with melancholy pertinacity, but equal want of success, enlarging the superscription with a thrice repeated *et cetera*. No man could care less than Washington for the empty parade of titles, but he did not of course choose to acquiesce in the intentional refusal to recognize him in the only capacity, in which Lord Howe was warranted to communicate with him at all.

By the several accessions alluded to, the British army was swelled to between twenty-five and thirty thousand well-appointed troops. The American army, in the aggregate, was numerically of almost equal size, but reduced by sickness, detachment, and absence on leave, to about eleven thousand men, fit for duty; and those not to be compared with efficient veteran soldiers. It was necessary that this small army should be widely distributed.

A considerable force was stationed at Brooklyn on Long Island, and the residue at various posts and forts on New York Island and the North and East Rivers. The head-quarters were in the city of New York. General Greene commanded on Long Island; but this able officer falling ill, his place was taken by General Sullivan. The enemy began to land detachments of troops on Long Island on the 22d of August, but it remained uncertain for some days where he would strike the main blow. On the 25th, General Putnam was ordered with a strong reinforcement to Brooklyn, where the following day was spent by the Commander-in-chief, in the necessary arrangements for the expected battle. On the 27th, a general action was fought, with greatly superior forces on the part of the enemy. The Americans were defeated with heavy loss, Generals Sullivan and Lord Stirling being among the prisoners.

General Howe encamped for the night in front of the position of the Americans, expecting no doubt to follow up his success the next day by their total rout. He probably overrated their strength; the day was rainy, and no forward movement was made by the British army on the 28th. In the course of that day an activity prevailed on Staten Island, which was thought to threaten an attempt on the city; and during the night, under cover of a dense fog, a masterly retreat, conducted by General Washington in person, was commenced, and before morning the entire American force on Long Island was brought off in safety. The battle of Long Island was one of the most disastrous events of the war; and the undiscovered retreat of the troops, within hearing of the hostile sentries, one of its most brilliant achievements. On these two eventful days Washington was for nearly forty-eight hours in the saddle, during which he did not close his eyes.

The greatly superior numbers of the royal army, and the control of the waters on which New York stands, compelled the retreat of the Americans, successively from the city and island of New York; and at the close of October, Washington occupied an intrenched camp at White Plains, a strong position about midway between the Hudson and East River. Here a pretty severe but partial action took place, which resulted favorably to the British. A general engagement seemed in prospect; but Sir William Howe (lately decorated with the order of the Bath) thought the position of Washington, who had withdrawn to higher ground, too strong to be forced, and concentrated his own troops at Harlem and on the Hudson, with the evident design of crossing into New Jersey, and marching on Philadelphia. To anticipate this movement Washington, after despatching Heath with a detachment to hold the Highlands, and leaving Lee in command near White Plains, crossed into New Jersey with the troops belonging to the states west of the Hudson. Lee, in whose military capacity and fidelity to the American cause too much confidence was reposed, was directed to remain at White Plains, or to follow the Commander-in-chief, as the exigencies of the service might require.

Fort Washington, a strong post on the Hudson, commanded by Colonel Magaw, was immediately invested by the British, and the garrison, amounting to over three thousand men, capitulated. This was another most disastrous blow to the American cause. Lord Cornwallis was immediately despatched into New Jersey with six thousand men; and, to prevent Sir William Howe from marching on Philadelphia with his entire army, Washington was compelled to retreat from river to river through that state. His numbers were much reduced by the loss of the garrison at Fort Washington, by the detachment of Heath to the Highlands, and the unpardonable tardiness of Lee in obeying the repeated orders of the Commander-in-chief to join the main body of the army. The further pernicious effects of his insubordination were prevented, after his arrival at Morristown, in New Jersey, by his surprise and capture, in the night, by a party of the enemy who had received a hint of his whereabout. This event, discreditable to himself, was hardly to be regretted by Washington, whom he was secretly plotting to undermine, and whom he omitted no opportunity to disparage. The Commander-in-chief crossed the Delaware River with barely four thousand troops. He was soon joined by other detachments of the army, but was in no condition to defend Philadelphia, if Sir William Howe, at the head of a large and well-appointed army, should, as soon as the Delaware was frozen, cross the ice, and attempt the city by assault.

The state and prospects of the American Army and cause were at this time more gloomy than at any other period of the war. The army, feeble and poorly provided at best, was on the point of dissolution by the expiration of its term of enlistment. The year 1776 and the campaign were closing amidst universal despondency. Washington almost alone remained unshaken; and, on one occasion, declared that if the enemy succeeded in obtaining possession of the whole of the Atlantic states, he would retreat behind the Alleghanies, and bid them defiance there. But it was precisely at this juncture that he struck the boldest stroke of the war, and, in less than two weeks, not only changed the entire face of affairs, and retrieved the fortunes of the campaign, but established his own reputation as a consummate chieftain.

A detachment of the royal army, consisting principally of the Hessian mercenaries, but with a squadron of British dragoons, had been pushed to the Delaware River, and occupied Trenton. Smaller bodies of royal troops were stationed at other points down the river; a still larger force was posted at Brunswick. Washington conceived the plan of crossing the Delaware, and surprising the Hessians at Trenton, and the other corps at Burlington and Bordentown. This was to

be effected by dividing his own small
force into three parties, which should
pass the river above and below Trenton,
headed respectively by himself, Cadwal-
ader, and Ewing. On the night of the
25th of December, when the Delaware, a
broad and rapid stream, was filled with
floating ice, under a driving storm alternately of snow, rain, and sleet, and with
the weather so cold that two of his men
froze to death by the way, his own part
of the movement was successfully accomplished. Trenton was surprised by him
about 8 o'clock in the morning; and after
a brief action, with nominal loss to the
Americans, a thousand Hessians were tak-
en prisoners, — their commander, Colonel
Rall, being killed. The dragoons escaped
down the river; and, owing to the impossibility of crossing it, — the masses of drift-
ice having become too fixed for the boats
to pass through, — the other portions of

the plan failed. Washington recrossed the Delaware in safety with his prisoners, who were nearly half as numerous as his own detachment, and, after an interval of two or three days, returned with his disposable force to the left bank of the river to resume the offensive.

Lord Cornwallis, who was on the eve of sailing for England, considering the campaign as closed, was detained by Sir William Howe, and sent in haste to Trenton, to arrest the progress of Washington. The latter, who had stationed himself behind the Assanpink, knowing the great inferiority of his force, decamped in the night from the bank of that river, and, forcing a march on Princeton, surprised a detachment of the royal army which was on the way to reinforce Cornwallis at Trenton. A sharp action ensued, in which Washington, as has been already stated, informed Colonel Trumbull, who painted a picture of the scene, that he was in greater personal danger than on any other occasion in his life, not excepting Braddock's defeat. The royal force was defeated with great loss both in killed and prisoners. Many also fell on the American side; among them the gallant and lamented Mercer.

By these bold and successful operations, the fortune of the war was completely reversed. All thoughts of moving on Philadelphia were for the present abandoned by Sir William Howe, and he confined himself for the rest of the winter to the positions occupied by his troops at New York, Amboy, and Brunswick. General Washington went into winter-quarters at Morristown, and the authority of Congress was restored throughout New Jersey, except in the places in the actual occupation of the British troops. These brilliant results, achieved at the moment of accumulated disaster and almost of despair, revived the confidence of the country, and earned for Washington a brilliant reputation as a strategist in the estimation of Europe.

CHAPTER VI.

Campaign of 1777 — Sir William Howe sails from Staten Island and ascends the Chesapeake — The Battle of Brandywine adverse to the Americans — Sir W. Howe occupies Philadelphia — Battle of Germantown — Capitulation of Burgoyne — Washington in Winter-Quarters at Valley Forge — The Gates and Conway Cabal — Forged Letters — Campaign of 1778 — The French Alliance — Sir W. Howe evacuates Philadelphia — Battle of Monmouth — Lee sentenced by a Court-Martial, and leaves the Army — The Count d'Estaing with a French Fleet arrives in the American Waters — Campaign of 1779 — No general Operation of the Main Body — Campaign of 1780 — Arrival of the First Division of the French Army under Rochambeau — Treason of Arnold — Fate of André — Campaign of 1781 — Arrival of Count de Grasse with Reinforcements — Capitulation of Cornwallis at Yorktown — Negotiations for Peace — Provisional Articles signed November, 1782 — Discontents in the American Army — The Newburg Address — Definitive Treaty of Peace — Washington resigns his Commission to the Congress at Annapolis, 23d December, 1783.

WITH the opening of the campaign of 1777, Sir William Howe, at the head of a vastly superior force, in vain endeavored to draw Washington into a general engagement. Burgoyne entered Canada, and the American commander was for some time at a loss what might be Sir William's ulterior plan of operations. It soon appeared that Philadelphia was his object; but not deeming it safe to march through New Jersey with the American army on his flanks and rear, Sir William hastily embarked his troops at Staten Island, and went round by sea to Chesapeake Bay. As soon as the news reached Washington that the royal fleet was seen at the Capes of the Delaware, he moved on Germantown, and thence to Chester.

It was at this time that Lafayette was introduced to the Commander-in-chief; and notwithstanding the caution with which foreigners were necessarily received, he was immediately taken into the confidence of Washington, which he justly retained to the end of his life. Serving as the medium of communication between the two countries, and possessing influence with both, the connection of Lafayette with the American Revolution contributed materially to its successful issue.

Sir William Howe ascended the Chesapeake Bay, and landed his army at the Head of Elk. Washington met him on the Brandywine with inferior numbers, and after a severe action, September 11th, in which Lafayette was wounded, the Americans were compelled to retreat. Notwithstanding this reverse, Washington succeeded, for eight or ten days, by skilful manœuvring and avoiding a general action, in keeping the royal army occupied; nor was it till the 22d of September that Sir William Howe was able to enter Philadelphia. A considerable detachment of his forces was stationed at Germantown. Washington, notwithstanding

the suffering condition of his army, after
a forced night march of seventeen miles,
on the 4th of October, attacked the royal
troops at Germantown,—and at first with
decided success. The fortune of the day,
in consequence of untoward circumstances,
turned against him; but the fact that he
was able so soon to resume the offensive,
was regarded, both at home and abroad,
as a proof of his unbroken spirit, and was
so spoken of by the Count de Vergennes,
in his communications with the American
commissioners at Paris.

In the meantime the success of Stark
at Bennington in Vermont, on the 16th
of August, had been followed by the
capitulation of the army of Burgoyne at
Saratoga, which took place a few days
after the affair at Germantown. This
capitulation was an all-important event in
its influence on the progress of the war;
but its immediate effect was unpropitious

to the reputation of the Commander-in-
chief, who was compelled, at the close of
the year, to place his army in a state
of almost total destitution in winter-quarters at Valley Forge. The brilliant success of General Gates at Saratoga, in
contrast with the reverses which had
befallen the American Army under the
immediate command of Washington, encouraged the operations of a cabal against
him, which had been formed by certain
disaffected officers of the army, and was
countenanced by a party in Congress.
The design was, by a succession of measures implying a want of confidence, to
drive Washington to retire from the service in disgust; and, when this object was
effected, to give the command of the
army to General Gates, who lent a willing ear to these discreditable intrigues.
A foreign officer in the American Army,
of the name of Conway, was the most

active promoter of the project, which was discovered by the accidental disclosure of a part of his correspondence with Gates. Washington bore himself on this occasion with his usual dignity, and allowed the parties concerned, in the army and in Congress, to take refuge in explanations, disclaimers, and apologies, by which those who made them gained no credit, and those who accepted them were not deceived.

A part of the machinery of this wretched cabal was the publication, in London, and the republication in New York, of the collection of forged letters already mentioned, bearing the name of Washington, and intended to prove his insincerity in the cause of the Revolution. Nothing perhaps more plainly illustrates his conscious strength of character, than the disdainful silence with which he allowed this miserable fabrication to remain for twenty years without exposure. It was only in the year 1796, and when about to retire from the Presidency, that he filed, in the department of State, a denial of its authenticity.

The year 1778 was one of great moment. Early in May, intelligence was received by Congress (which sat at Yorktown, in Pennsylvania, during the occupation of Philadelphia by Sir William Howe) that the American commissioners in Paris had negotiated treaties of alliance and commerce with France. It would be easy to prove, from the diplomatic correspondence of the day, that whatever credit is due to the skill with which the negotiations at Paris were conducted by Franklin, the confidence reposed by the French government in the character of Washington was a very great inducement for hazarding a step which involved, as its first consequence, a war with Great Britain.

Sir William Howe had gained nothing by the campaign of 1777, though it had resulted in the temporary possession of Philadelphia. The occupation of that city was barren of results; the ministry were dissatisfied with his conduct of the war, and he resigned his command. Sir Henry Clinton was appointed in his place; and an expedition against the French possessions in the West Indies being determined upon by the ministry, a strong force was detached for that purpose from the royal army in America. The evacuation of Philadelphia, after eight months' occupation, was the first step in the new plan of campaign. Having shipped his cavalry, his German troops, the American loyalists, and his heavy baggage, to go round by sea, Sir Henry marched for New York with the main body of his troops, across New Jersey. Washington immediately started with his newly organized army in pursuit, and in six days was on the left bank of the Delaware. He was desirous of bringing the royal army to a general engagement; but the council of war called by him was divided on the expediency of the measure. General Lee, who had been exchanged for the British General Prescott and was now second in command, vehemently opposed it. Washington, however, determined to assume the responsibility of the measure; and having overtaken Sir Henry near Monmouth, sent forward Lafayette, and afterwards Lee, with a strong advance, to engage the royal army. Hastening himself to their support, he encountered Lee in full retreat at the head of five thousand men. This retrograde movement was arrested by Washington, and the engagement vigorously renewed. The close of the day put an end to the conflict; but Washington passed the night with his army on the field, determined to renew the action the following morning. Sir Henry, however, continued his march, undiscovered, during the night, and in the morning was out of reach. This engagement, though hardly to be called a victory, was a decided advantage on the part of Washington. In his own words, "from an unfortunate and bad beginning, it turned out a glorious and happy day." His loss was far inferior to that acknowledged by Sir Henry Clinton. The British army pursued its march to New York, and Washington, crossing the Hudson, resumed his former position at White Plains.

The day after the battle of Monmouth, a correspondence took place between Lee and Washington, which resulted in the trial of the former by a court-martial. The charges were disobedience of orders, an unnecessary, disorderly, and shameful retreat, and language disrespectful to the

Commander-in-chief. The court spared him the epithet of "shameful;" but found him guilty of the rest of the charges, and suspended him from his command for a twelvemonth. He left the army never to return, and died before the close of the war, at Philadelphia. Washington's heroic patience was never more signally displayed than in tolerating as he did, from public motives, for three years, the arrogant pretensions of this coarse and empty braggart, whom recent discoveries have proved also to have been a concealed traitor to the American cause.*

In the course of the summer the Count d'Estaing, with fourteen sail of the line, arrived in the American waters, and a combined expedition was undertaken, but

* The Treason of Lee is placed beyond doubt, and the original documents establishing it are published in the recent highly valuable monograph of G. H. Moore, Esq., on that subject.

without success, against the royal forces in Newport. Causes of dissatisfaction arose between the American officers in command in Rhode Island and the Count d'Estaing, —but the mediating influence of Washington was exerted, with consummate skill, to avert the consequences. His headquarters were established at Fredericksburg, in New York, about thirty miles from West Point, and the campaign closed without further events of importance.

The year 1779 passed without any general engagement of the main army of Washington. A very extensive expedition against Canada had been projected in Congress; but it was not favored by the French government, and was wholly discountenanced by Washington. The summer was employed by the British army in predatory excursions. On the American side, a brilliant success was gained by General Wayne at Stony

Point. The British fleet followed Count
d'Estaing to the West Indies. Sir Henry
Clinton sailed with a strong detachment
to the Southern States; and at the close
of the season the army of General Washington went into winter-quarters. In the
course of the year a visit was made to
the Commander-in-chief, at his head-quarters, by M. Gerard, the French Minister,
who, in his report of their conference to
the Count de Vergennes, uses the following language: "I have had many conver-
sations with General Washington, some
of which have continued for three hours.
It is impossible for me briefly to communicate the fund of intelligence which
I have derived from him. . . I will
now say only, that I have formed as
high an opinion of the powers of his
mind, his moderation, his patriotism, and
his virtues, as I had before conceived,
from common report, of his military tal-

ent, and of the incalculable services which he has rendered his country."

Before the end of April, 1780, Lafayette returned to the United States from France, with the news that an auxiliary army would be despatched to the assistance of the Americans. On the 10th of July, the first division of the French fleet arrived at Newport, under the Chevalier de Ternay, having on board an army of five thousand men, commanded by the Count de Rochambeau. A second division was to follow, but was blockaded at Brest. The superiority both by land and by sea accordingly remained on the side of the British, by whom Count de Rochambeau's army was blockaded in Newport. In consequence of this state of things, no expedition of magnitude was attempted by the allies in the course of the year 1780.

It was during the absence of Wash-

ington at Hartford, to confer with the
Count de Rochambeau, on a plan of
operations for the ensuing campaign, that
the treason of Arnold was discovered,
and the arrest and execution of the unfortunate Major André took place.   It
would exceed the limits of these pages to
enter into a narrative of this event, or
to engage in the defence of Washington,
against the reproaches cast upon him, for
approving the sentence of the court by
which the case was adjudicated.   It is
sufficient to say that this unfortunate officer was condemned as a spy by a court
of thirteen officers native and foreign,
some of them the most intelligent in the
service.   Those who condemn Washington
for not placing his *veto* on their sentence,
should ask themselves, what would probably have been the fate of an English
officer, who should have been discovered
in citizen's dress, within the lines of the

French army at Boulogne in 1803; or of a French officer who, under similar circumstances, should have been caught within the English lines at Gibraltar, in time of war, plotting with a traitor for the surrender of an important post. It may be doubted whether retribution, in either case, would have awaited the slow motions of a court. André's execution as a spy has been condemned on the ground that, at the time of his arrest, he had a free pass from an American general, as if it were an apology for a spy, that he was in conspiracy with a traitor. Washington is liberally " acquitted of all injustice " towards André, in a memoir by Mr. Locker, who, as the friend of Major André's sisters, superintended the interment of their brother's remains in Westminster Abbey.* Personally General Washington was the most hu-

* Knight's *Popular History of England*, vol. vi. p. 416.

13

mane of men; and it is well known that it cost him a painful struggle with his feelings, to allow the sentence of the court to be executed on the accomplished prisoner. But with respect to him, it is scarcely necessary to say, that there was nothing in his errand, to increase the respect and sympathy, inspired by his personal qualities and unhappy fate.

But the great struggle was drawing to a close more rapidly than was anticipated. The year 1781 witnessed the last military operations of decided importance. The Count de Grasse having arrived in the Chesapeake from the West Indies with a commanding fleet and a considerable reinforcement of troops, Washington and Rochambeau immediately marched from the Hudson to Virginia, to join forces with Lafayette, who was stationed at Williamsburg to watch the movements of Lord Cornwallis. On the approach of the combined French and American armies, Lord Cornwallis intrenched himself at Yorktown. That place was invested in form on the 30th of September by the allied army. The outposts were in a few days carried by assault; and on the 19th of October the army of Cornwallis, rather more than seven thousand strong, capitulated to the united and greatly superior forces of the allies.

This brilliant success put an end to the contest, and General Washington had the satisfaction of seeing the war brought to a close, under his own immediate auspices and command. Negotiations for peace commenced at Paris in the summer of 1782, and the articles of a provisional treaty were signed in November of that year. Attempts were made by further negotiation, in the course of the ensuing year, to enlarge the stipulations agreed upon, but the definitive treaty was eventually signed at Paris on the 3d of September, 1783, in the words of the provisional articles.

After the surrender of Yorktown and the departure of Count de Rochambeau's army, General Washington established his head-quarters at Newburg, on the Hudson River. Here the American Army, in the now certain prospect of peace, justly dissatisfied with the want of all provision to give effect to the resolution of October, 1780, by which half-pay for life was promised to the officers, endeavored by a new appeal to Congress, to obtain a definitive settlement of their claims, by an equitable commutation. Congress was divided on the expediency of the measure; and, if it had been unanimous, possessed no power to give effect to its recommendations. Vague promises were made, but nothing effective done. Great irritation arose on the return of the delegates to head-quarters A meeting of the officers was called, and an inflammatory appeal to the army was circulated, celebrated as *The Newburg Address*, " in which the troops were exhorted not to allow themselves to be disbanded till justice was obtained." It was a moment of great alarm and real danger, but the influence of the Commander-in-chief, official and personal, was promptly called into action, and moderate counsels prevailed.

So tardy were communications across the Atlantic at that time, that official information of the provisional treaty was not received in the United States till the spring of 1783, when it came by the way of Cadiz; and it was first officially proclaimed to the army on the 19th of April, 1783, the anniversary of the day on which, eight years before, the war commenced at Lexington and Concord. Furloughs were freely granted to officers and men from that time forward, and on the 18th of October the army was formally released from service. New York was surrendered by Sir Guy Carleton to General Washington on the 25th of November, and on the 4th of December the Commander-in-chief took an affectionate and pathetic leave of his brother officers. Repairing to Annapolis, to which place Congress had adjourned, General Washington, on the 23d of December, made his formal resignation in an address of surpassing beauty and dignity, which we quote at length : —

"MR. PRESIDENT,

"The great events on which my resignation depended, having at length taken place, I have now the honor of offering my sincere congratulations to Congress, and of presenting myself before them, to surrender into their hands the trust committed to me, and to claim the indulgence of retiring from the service of my country.

"Happy in the confirmation of our independence and sovereignty, and pleased with the opportunity afforded the United States of becoming a respectable nation, I resign with satisfaction the appointment I accepted with diffidence; a diffidence in my abilities to accomplish so arduous a task; which, however, was superseded by a confidence in the rectitude of our cause, the support of the supreme power of the Union, and the patronage of Heaven.

"The successful termination of the war has verified the most sanguine expectations; and my gratitude for the interposition of Providence, and the assistance I have received from my countrymen, increases with every review of the momentous contest.

"While I repeat my obligations to the army in general, I should do injustice to my own feelings not to acknowledge, in this place, the peculiar services and distinguished merits of the gentlemen who have been attached to my person during the war. It was impossible the choice of confidential officers to compose my family should have been more fortunate. Permit me, sir, to recommend in particular those who have continued in the service to the present moment, as worthy of the favorable notice and patronage of Congress.

"I consider it an indispensable duty to close this last act of my official life by commending the interests of our dearest country to the protection of Almighty God, and those who have the superintendence of them to His holy keeping.

"Having now finished the work assigned me, I retire from the great theatre of action, and bidding an affectionate farewell to this august body, under whose orders I have so long acted, I here offer my Commission, and take my leave of all the employments of public life."

CHAPTER VII.

Washington retires to Mount Vernon — Visits the Country west of the Alleghanies — Recommends opening a Communication between the Head Waters of the Atlantic Rivers and the Ohio — Agricultural Pursuits — His Views of Slavery — Critical State of the Country — Steps that led to the Formation of the present Government — The Federal Convention and Washington its President — The Constitution framed — Adopted by the States — Washington elected the First President of the United States, and inaugurated 30th of April, 1789.

IMMEDIATELY on resigning his commission General Washington returned to his home at Mount Vernon, which, during the eight years of the war, he had visited but twice, and then hastily, on his way to and from Yorktown in the year 1781, with the Count de Rochambeau. Greatly attached to his agricultural and horticultural pursuits, he devoted his time to the care of his plantations, garden, and grounds, — to the management of what was considered in America at that time a large landed property; to the extensive correspondence which devolved upon him, particularly in connection with the events of the war; and to the reception and entertainment of visitors, who came in great numbers from every part of the United States and from Europe. This last mentioned call upon his time and attention, necessarily very serious, was rendered less oppressive than it would otherwise have been, by the excellent housewifery of Mrs. Washington, who administered with method and skill the liberal but unostentatious hospitality of Mount Vernon. For two years after the war, he carried on his heavy correspondence without clerical aid, writing and copying his letters with his own hand. To the close of his life he kept his account-books with great care and with his own hand, according to the system of double entry.

In the autumn of 1784, General Washington crossed the Alleghanies, partly for the purpose of examining the lands which he had formerly taken up in that region, and partly to explore the head waters of the Potomac and James rivers, with reference to their connection with the streams which flow into the Ohio. This was a subject which had, from an early period, been familiar to his thoughts, as one of vast importance to the growth and prosperity of the United States. The result of his inquiries was highly favorable to a system of inland navigation, connecting the Atlantic seaboard with the great rivers of the West, and the region drained by them. On his return he addressed an elaborate, well-reasoned, and persuasive letter on the subject to the governor of Virginia. This communication had a powerful effect on the public mind, and led to the organization of the James River and Potomac Canal Companies. In acknowledgment of his agency in bringing about this result, and still more in gratitude for his Revolutionary services, the State of Virginia presented him with fifty shares in the Potomac Canal Company, valued at ten thousand dollars, and one hundred shares in the James River Canal Company, valued at fifty thousand dollars. In obedience to the principle which governed him through life, this grant was accepted by Washington only on condition, that he should be allowed to hold the property in trust for some public object. The shares in the James River Canal were finally appropriated for the endowment of a college at Lexington, in Rockbridge County, Virginia, which in consequence assumed the name of Washington College. The shares in the Potomac Canal Company were appropriated for the endowment of a university at the seat of the Federal Government,— an appropriation which remains without effect.

Agriculture was at this period of his life, as indeed at almost every period, his main occupation. He looked upon his official duties, civil and military, as an interruption to its pursuit. A resident in the lower part of Virginia, and the owner of extensive landed estates, he was, as a matter of course, a slaveholder. His correspondence shows him to have been a strict and vigilant, but at the same time a just, thoughtful, and humane master; studying his own interest in the cultivation of his farms, not more than the comfort and welfare of his dependants. In common with most, if not all, the leading statesmen of Virginia of that day, he was opposed to slavery; but he happily lived at a time when the subject, which now so violently agitates the American Union, had not yet been drawn into the party divisions of the country, and was discussed exclusively in its bearings on the public welfare. As early as 1786, he had formed a resolution never, unless compelled by particular circumstances, "to possess another slave by purchase;" and in a letter to Mr. Morris, written in that year, he says: "There is not a man living who wishes more sincerely than I do to see a plan adopted for the abolition of slavery. But there is only one proper and effectual mode by which it can be accomplished, and that is by legislative authority; and this, as far as my suffrage will go, will never be wanting." This sentiment is repeated in several parts of his correspondence; but his habitual respect for

the law led him to deprecate all interference with legal rights; and it is the
object of the letter to Mr. Morris, from
which the above extract is taken, to re-
monstrate, with reference to a particular
case, against such interference on the
part of "individuals and private societies." *

The period succeeding the peace of
1783, up to the adoption of the Constitution of the United States in 1788, was
more critical, with reference to the permanent prosperity of the country, than
that of the war itself, however oppressive
and exhausting. A reduction of the states,
which had declared themselves independent, to the former colonial condition, could
not have been brought about by continu-
ing the war; but the peace found the
United States without a government, —
unable to command respect abroad, or to

* Sparks's *Washington*, vol. ix. p. 158.

start upon a career of prosperous growth and development at home. The country was exhausted by the war; there were no manufactures, very little commerce, and no means, except recommendations of the Congress of the Confederation, (which were treated with utter neglect,) of raising a revenue for the purpose either of paying the interest of the foreign debt, or to meet any public expenditure for domestic purposes. The manifold evils of this state of things were felt by every intelligent person, but the remedy was all but hopeless. The most obvious resort was to clothe the Federal Congress with the power to raise a revenue by imposts and direct taxation. But there was, on the part of some of the states, a great reluctance to confer larger powers on that body; and few even of the most far-sighted individuals had conceived the idea of converting the old confederation, which was simply a league of independent states, assembled in Congress, each with equal powers, and acting only by recommendations addressed to their separate state governments, into a federal government possessing authority that should bind the individual citizen. This change, however, was at length effected, and by a series of agencies, at first in striking disproportion to the importance of the result, and in no small degree under the influence of Washington. Although wholly retired to private life, his name and authority were at this time almost the only vital power in the country; the common respect and reverence for him almost the only bond of union.

It will be borne in mind, that before the adoption of the present Constitution of the United States, the several states were, in all their commercial affairs, in the relation to each other of independent nations; and it happened in some instances that conterminous states pursued a policy of mutual hostility. In the month of March, 1785, commissioners on the part of Maryland and Virginia met at Alexandria, in the latter state, for the purpose of "keeping up harmony in the commercial regulations of the two states, with reference to the navigation of the rivers Potomac and Pocomoke, and of the Chesapeake Bay," the waters of which were to some extent common to the two states. General Washington was one of the commissioners on the part of Virginia; and his associates being on a visit to him at Mount Vernon, it was there agreed by them to recommend to their respective states the appointment of a new commission, with enlarged powers, to devise a plan for the establishment, under the sanction of Congress, of a naval force on the Chesapeake Bay, and a uniform tariff of duties on imports, to which the laws of the two states should conform. The proposal, thus concerted at Mount Vernon, was adopted by the legislature of Virginia; and being brought before that body at a time when it had under consideration a project for granting enlarged commercial powers to Congress, a resolution was passed, directing that so much of the report of the commissioners as referred to a uniform tariff of duties should be communicated to the other states, with an invitation to attend the proposed meeting. On the 21st of January, 1786, a resolution passed the legislature of Virginia, appointing commissioners to meet with those which might be appointed by the other states, " to take into consideration the trade of the United States; to examine the relative situation and trade of the said states; to consider how far a uniform system in their commercial regulations may be necessary to their common interest and their permanent harmony." Washington, at his own instance for personal reasons, was not a member of this commission, though the object was one which he had greatly at heart. The meeting was appointed to be held in Annapolis, in September, 1786; but delegates from five states only attended, and some of them with powers too limited for any valuable purpose. Nothing accordingly was attempted beyond the preparation of a report, setting forth the existing evils, and recommending to the several states to appoint delegates to meet at Philadelphia the next May. A copy of this report was sent to the Congress of the Confederation, which still retained a nominal existence; and that body, by recommending the proposed measure, gave it, in the opinion of some persons, that necessary constitutional sanction, in which the meeting at Annapolis was deficient. This report was adopted by Virginia, and seven delegates appointed, with Washington at their head, to represent that state in the proposed convention.

This body, now usually called the "Federal Convention," assembled in Philadelphia on the 2d of May, 1787. Washington was unanimously elected its president. In anticipation of the meeting and the duties which might devolve upon its members, "he read," says Mr. Sparks, "the history, and examined the principles, of the ancient and modern confederacies. There is a paper in his handwriting, which contains an abstract of each, and in which are noted, in a methodical order, their chief characteristics, the kinds of authority they possessed, their modes of operation, and their defects. The confederacies analyzed in this paper are the Lycian,

Amphictyonic, Achæan, Helvetic, Belgic, and Germanic." The debates in the convention were principally had in committee of the whole, in which, by the appointment of Washington as the presiding officer of the body, the chair was occupied by the Hon. Nathaniel Gorham, of Massachusetts. Without his taking an active part in the debates, the influence of Washington was steadily exerted, and in the direction of an efficient central government. The convention remained in session about four months; and on the 17th of September, 1787, the result of their labors, as embodied in the present Constitution of the United States, was communicated to the Federal Congress, with a letter signed by General Washington, as president of the convention. This instrument of government, under which the United States have so signally prospered for nearly three fourths of a century, though not deemed perfect in every point by Washington, or probably by any of its most ardent friends, was regarded by him, and declared to be, in his correspondence, the best that could be hoped for in the condition of the country, and as presenting the only alternative for anarchy and civil war. "There is a tradition," says Mr. George T. Curtis, in his valuable "History of the Constitution," * " that when Washington was about to sign the instrument, he rose from his seat, and holding the pen in his hand, after a short pause, pronounced these words: 'Should the states reject this excellent constitution, the probability is that an opportunity will never again be offered to cancel another in peace,— the next will be drawn in blood.'"

The convention, by which the Constitution was framed, was not clothed with

* Vol. ii. p. 487.

legislative power, nor was the Congress of the Confederation competent to accept or reject the new form of government. It was referred by them to the several states, represented by conventions of the people; and it was provided in the instrument itself, that it should become the supreme law of the land, when adopted by nine states. The residue of the year 1787, and the first half of 1788 were taken up with the holding of these conventions, and it was not till the summer of 1788 that the ratification of nine states was obtained. The action of these conventions was watched with great solicitude by Washington, and his influence was efficiently employed, through the medium of his correspondence, to procure the adoption of the new form of government.

The 4th of March, 1789, had been appointed by the Congress, as the time when the new Constitution should go into operation. Previous to that time, the choice of the electoral colleges, and of the senators and representatives who were to compose the first Congress, was to be had in the several states. By the Constitution, as originally framed, two persons were to be voted for by the presidential electors, as president and vice-president, without designating for which of the two offices the candidates were respectively supported. The candidate receiving the majority of votes was to be the president; and in case of equality of two or more candidates, the House of Representatives, voting not *per capita* but by states, the members from each state, whether great or small, casting one vote, was to designate a president and vice-president, from the five highest candidates having an equal number of votes. The whole number of electoral votes given in the first election was but sixty-nine, and they were all for General Washington. Thirty-four votes were given for John Adams, and a much smaller number of votes being scattered among several other candidates, George Washington and John Adams were elected the first President and Vice-President of the United States. The private and confidential correspondence of Washington shows the sincerity of his uniform public declarations, that he shrunk from the office with unaffected reluctance, both as a candidate and after his election. He is probably the only person who has ever been called to the chair of state, without having desired, and to some extent perhaps exerted himself to obtain, the nomination.

Such was the apathy of the country with reference to the new form of government, and such the tardiness of the new Congress in coming together, that although the 4th of March, 1789, was appointed as the day of meeting, a quorum of the two Houses was not assembled till the 6th of April. The first business was to count the electoral votes for president and vice-president, and to communicate the result to the persons chosen. Washington received the official notification of his election at Mount Vernon, on the 14th of April, and started immediately for the seat of government, which was for the first two years established at New York. His journey through the states of Maryland, Pennsylvania, and New Jersey, was a triumphal procession. Debates in Congress on the proper official style by which he was to be addressed, and a disagreement between the two Houses on that subject, which ended in nothing being done, caused some delay; and it was not till the 30th of April, 1789, that he took the oath prescribed by the constitution, as the first President of the United States. There were other statesmen in the country who stood high in the respect and in the affections of the people; but the preference for Washington was absolute and unqualified. No other individual was thought of for a moment as a rival candidate. In advance of all the constitutional forms of election, which in his case were but forms, he was chosen unanimously in the hearts of the people. He was fifty-seven years old when he entered upon the office. His frame was naturally vigorous and athletic, but its strength was perhaps somewhat impaired by the labors and exposures of two wars, and by repeated severe attacks of disease. Such an attack threatened his life immediately after entering upon the presidency; and in a letter to Lafayette he speaks of himself, at the age of fifty-one, as having inherited the constitution of a short-lived family. His father died young, but his venerable mother lived to witness his elevation to the presidency, and died at the age of eighty-two. Washington had made a farewell visit to her before repairing to the seat of government. His great elevation and distinguished honors produced no change in her simple mode of life. She occupied, to the last, the humble dwelling of one upright story at Fredericksburg, in which she had passed so many years, and which, somewhat modernized, is still standing. Her habitual commendation of him was, that " George had always been a good son."

CHAPTER VIII.

Washington's Administration continued through two Terms of Office — Peculiar Difficulties at Home and Abroad — Tendency toward the Formation of Parties — The Cabinet divided — Growth of Party-Spirit — Washington unanimously reëlected — Retirement of Jefferson and Hamilton from the Cabinet—War between France and England — Neutrality of the United States — Violated by both the Belligerents — Offensive Proceedings of Genet, the French Minister — Mission of Jay to England — His Treaty unpopular — Attempt in the House of Representatives to withhold the Appropriations to carry it into Effect — Washington refuses to communicate the Instructions under which it was negotiated.

At the close of his first presidential term of four years, though extremely desirous of retiring from public life, he yielded to the urgency of friends of all parties, and consenting to accept the office for a second period, was again unanimously elected. His administration, therefore, may be spoken of as covering a space of eight years, from the date of the new government. As that government was, in its leading features, a new political system, and all its departments were to be organized and put in action for the first time, unusual difficulties attended his administration, for the want of precedents to which he could look for guidance. Other difficulties grew out of the state of public affairs abroad and at home. The interest felt in the American Revolution by the friends of liberty in Europe had to a considerable degree passed away, and the United States had not acquired a strength which enabled them to command the respect of foreign powers. Worse than this, it was some time before a fiscal system could be organized, and a revenue raised for paying the interest of the foreign debt, — a debt paltry in amount, but no debt is small which a man is unable to pay. Difficulties arose with England, relative to the execution of the treaty of 1783, by which the independence of the United States was acknowledged. She complained that the states threw obstacles in the way of the recovery of debts due to British subjects; and the United States in turn complained that the military posts on the northwestern frontier were retained by England, and the Indians encouraged in their hostility against the Union. Soon the French Revolution broke out; and each of the belligerents gave great cause of complaint to the American government. Meantime, important questions and interests divided opinion and gradually led to the formation of parties at home: the assumption by Congress of the revolutionary debts of the states; the funding system; the location of the seat of the federal government; the taxes to which resort had been had to create a revenue; the establishment of a national bank; and, as the French Revolution advanced, the relations of the Union to the two great belligerents.

At the commencement of his administration, and before the organization of the parties which afterwards took place, General Washington surrounded himself, in the executive offices, with the most distinguished men in the country. Mr. Jefferson in the department of state and Mr. Hamilton in the treasury, the prospective leaders of the two great parties into which the country was before long divided, received equal marks of his confidence; and when his retirement from office at the end of the first term was proposed by him, they, with equal urgency, entreated him to accept a re-nomination. Had it been possible for any person to administer the presidential office without the aid of party support, or rather to conciliate unanimous support by merits and services, which win the respect and gratitude of all parties, Washington was certainly marked out by the entire course of his life and the history of the country as such a person. It was his earnest desire to give this character to his administration. He had composed it of the individuals who, in different parts of the Union, possessed most of the public confidence, and whom he had called to his assistance on the sole ground of being best qualified to conduct the public business to the satisfaction of the people. But the administration of a government, and especially one coming into existence, where much of the detail of organization is to be struck out anew, necessarily assumes a certain leading character founded on general principles and ideas, with respect to which the judg-

ments of men naturally differ. It is only
in times of extreme peril, and hardly
then, that they can be brought to think
alike and act in one united mass, without
party divisions.

General Washington's administration
commenced with a state of public opinion predisposed to the formation of parties. The constitution had been adopted,
in the most important states, by slender
majorities, and in the face of a strong
opposition. Those who opposed the adoption of the constitution were, generally
speaking, persons who regarded a strong
central government with apprehension, as
dangerous to the prerogatives of the
state governments and the liberties of
the people. It was a matter of course
that, after the adoption of the constitution, the measures of the new government, which tended to give it strength
and efficiency, should be feared and op-

posed by the same class of statesmen and citizens. Among these measures were some which, by their friends, were deemed of vital importance to the government of the country, such as the funding system, the assumption of the revolutionary debts of the several states, and the establishment of a national bank. On these measures the members of the first Cabinet were divided. Mr. Hamilton, the secretary of the treasury, by whom they were proposed, and Knox, the secretary of war, were on one side; Mr. Jefferson, the secretary of state, and Mr. Randolph, the attorney-general, on the other. The political influences throughout the country were about equally divided, Mr. Hamilton and Mr. Jefferson being respectively the acknowledged representatives of the systems, which favored and opposed a strong central government. General Washington, with untiring assiduity and patience, sought to conciliate the opposite opinions, holding himself in suspense, as long as the public service admitted, as to the adoption of particular measures, and seeking advice with equal anxiety on both sides. Eventually, however, a decision must be made; the measure is a distinct political issue and must be adopted or rejected. In reference to the subjects above referred to, the President sustained the general views of the secretary of the treasury; and in this way, though standing aloof from all electioneering plans and arrangements, became at length identified in public opinon with the principles and measures of the party of which Mr. Hamilton was the acknowledged leader. His great name and spotless character shielded him, for a considerable time, from the assaults of party warfare. The persons that opposed his administration were content with condemning its measures and inveighing against those members of the Cabinet and of Congress by whom they were projected and sustained. Some check was imposed on all general censures upon his administration, so long as Mr. Jefferson remained at the head of it, and responsible even for some of the measures most obnoxious to its opponents, such as the proclamation of neutrality in the war between France and England. All restraint of this kind ceased with his retirement from the Cabinet soon after the commencement of his second term. That of Mr. Hamilton took place not long afterward. But the withdrawal of these great rivals, instead of relieving Washington from the embarrassments arising from their hostile relations to each other, was in fact the signal for a stricter organization, in Congress and throughout the country, of the parties of which they were severally the leaders.

Mr. Hamilton was understood to carry with him more of the confidence and sympathy of the President, who was from that time more and more identified in public opinion with the federal, which was still the dominant, party. Party defamation, however, reached him only by slow degrees, and, if one may use that phrase, with moderation. He possessed a hold on the affections of the country too strong to be seriously loosened by newspaper diatribes. It was notorious to the whole people, that office, so far from being an object of his ambition, was regarded by him as a burden. His revolutionary services were still everywhere freshly and enthusiastically appreciated. Men of high character, though opposed to his political system, desired to treat him personally with respect; vulgar detraction could not reach him. Accordingly, though parties might be considered

as distinctly organized by the close of
the first term of his administration, he
was, as we have stated, unanimously re-
elected, having received one hundred and
thirty-two votes, in the electoral colleges,
— that being the entire number of the
presidential electors.

In the first year of his administration,
the President made a hasty tour through
the Eastern States of the Union; and, in
the following spring, he visited the Southern States,—on each occasion (it is mentioned as a trait of manners) travelling
with his own carriage and horses. The
United States at that time numbered a
population of about four millions; the
largest cities, Philadelphia, Boston, and
New York, were then small towns; the
great branches of industry were almost
unknown; a small military force guarded
the Indian frontier; there was not a single
public vessel; nor a state government

west of the Alleghanies. This state of things but ill sustains the comparison with that which we now behold in the American Union: thirty-three states, some of the largest in the basin of the Mississippi, and two on the Pacific Ocean; a population of thirty millions; a commercial tonnage inferior to that of England alone, if inferior even to that; a highly advanced condition of the great industrial pursuits; a respectable military and naval establishment; and creditable progress in science and literature. Yet the United States, as Washington saw them on his tours in 1789 and 1790, presented such a contrast with the colonies as he traversed them on his way to Boston in 1756, as was probably never brought within the experience of one man, and within so narrow a compass as thirty-three years.

Washington entered upon his second

term of the presidential office, to which, as we have seen, he had been unanimously re-elected, on the 3d of March, 1793. He still stood before the country with unshaken personal popularity, in a relation unshared, indeed unapproached by any other individual, but at length was driven by the force of circumstances, and strongly against his private impulses, into the position of the head of an administration, which, if warmly supported, was also warmly opposed. Shortly after the commencement of his second term of office, the war between France and England broke out. The French revolution, as was natural from the all-important services rendered by France to the United States in their own revolutionary struggle, enlisted the warm sympathy of the American people. Washington fully shared this sentiment, and his great personal regard for Lafayette, with whom he kept up a regular correspondence, and from whom he naturally derived his general impressions of the march of events, led him to look with a favorable eye upon the movements, of which Lafayette was for a considerable time an influential leader. But that judicial moderation, which was the most striking trait of Washington's character, soon took alarm at the excesses of the French revolution, and the conclusions of his own mind were confirmed by the tenor of the despatches of Mr. Gouverneur Morris, who, as the American minister at Paris, enjoyed much of the confidence of Louis the Sixteenth and his family, and of the still faithful friends of the tottering monarchy.

As the United States were first introduced to the family of nations by the alliance with France of 1778, the very important question arose, on the breaking out of the war between France and

England, how far they were bound to take part in the contest. The second article of the treaty of alliance seemed to limit its operation to the then existing war between the United States and Great Britain; but by the eleventh article the two contracting powers agreed to "guarantee mutually from the present time and *forever*, against all other powers," the territories of which the allies might be in possession respectively at the moment the war between France and Great Britain should break out, which was anticipated as the necessary consequence of the alliance.

Not only were the general sympathies of America strongly with France, but the course pursued by Great Britain toward the United States, since the peace of 1783, was productive of extreme irritation, especially her refusal to give up the western posts, which, as has been intimated, had the effect of involving the northwestern frontier in a prolonged and disastrous Indian war. These causes, together with the recent recollections of the revolutionary struggle, disposed the popular mind to make common cause with France, in what was regarded as the war of a people struggling for freedom against the combined despots of Europe. Washington, however, from the first, determined to maintain the neutrality of the country. The news of the war reached him at Mount Vernon, and he immediately addressed letters to the heads of department, to prepare them to express their opinions, on his return to the seat of government, as to the measures necessary to prevent the country from being drawn into the vortex. They agreed unanimously on the expediency of issuing a proclamation of neutrality, and of receiving a minister from the

French republic; while on some other points submitted to them, especially the extent of the above-mentioned " guaranty," the members of the Cabinet were equally divided.

This proclamation, though draughted by Mr. Jefferson and unanimously adopted by the Cabinet, was violently assailed by the organs of the party which followed his lead. A series of questions which General Washington had confidentially submitted to the Cabinet; embracing all the phases of the relations between the two countries, had found its way to the public, and the President was assumed to have answered in his own mind, adversely to France, every question proposed by him for the opinion of his constitutional advisers. The growing excitement of the popular mind was fanned to a flame by the arrival at Charleston, South Carolina, of " Citizen " Genet, whc was sent as the minister of the French Republic to the United States. Without repairing to the seat of government, or being accredited in any way, in his official capacity, he began to fit out privateers in Charleston, to cruise against the commerce of England. Although the utmost gentleness and patience were observed by the executive of the United States in checking this violation of their neutrality, Genet assumed from the first a tone of defiance, and threatened before long to appeal from the government to the people. These insolent demonstrations were of course lost upon Washington's firmness and moral courage. They distressed, but did not in the slightest degree intimidate him; and their effect on the popular mind was to some extent neutralized by the facts, that the chief measures to maintain the neutrality of the country had been unanimously adviscd by the Cabinet, and that the duty of rebuking his intemperate course had devolved upon the secretary of state, the recognized head of the party to which Genet looked for sympathy.

If the conduct of France and of the French minister gave great offence to the American government, that of England was scarcely less exceptionable. Besides the causes of irritation already mentioned, she had added materially to the existing animosity by orders in council, by which the lawful carrying-trade of the United States was vexatiously interfered with, and still more by the impressment of seamen from our vessels. At the close of the first year of President Washington's second administration, a very able and elaborate report was drawn up by Mr. Jefferson, then about to retire from office, on the commercial relations of the country. At the session of Congress

17

of 1794, a discrimination against the commerce of England was proposed in a series of resolutions introduced by Mr. Madison, the leader of the opposition in the House of Representatives, and a statesman whose general moderation was not less conspicuous than his ability and patriotism. Proportionate weight attached to a measure brought forward under his advocacy. The subject was debated in various forms in the course of the session, and an act passed the House of Representatives embracing the principle of discrimination, which was, however, lost in the Senate, by the casting vote of the vice-president.

In this critical state of affairs, General Washington determined to take a decisive step to extricate the country from the embarrassment of being at variance, at the same time, with both of the belligerents. This step was the appointment of a special minister to England; and the selection for this important trust of the chief justice of the United States, John Jay, one of the wisest and most circumspect, as well as one of the most experienced, of the public men of the day. His nomination was violently assailed by the opposing party, and barely passed the Senate. He succeeded in negotiating a treaty, by which the principal points in controversy between the two governments were settled: the western posts were given up; indemnification promised by the United States for the losses accruing by the non-payment of debts due to British creditors, and by Great Britain for illegal captures; and the commercial intercourse of the two nations was in most respects satisfactorily regulated. The twelfth article failed to obtain the confirmation of the Senate, inasmuch as it stipulated that molasses, sugar, coffee, cocoa, and *cotton,* should not be carried in American vessels, either from the British islands or from the United States, to any foreign port; the great agricultural staple of the country, of which more than four millions of bales will be exported the present year (1860), not being known, sixty-five years ago, to the negotiators on either side as an article of American production!

On the arrival and before the official promulgation of the treaty, it was violently assailed. It was barely adopted by the constitutional majority (two thirds) of the Senate, and on its official publication became the subject of unmeasured denunciation. Boston led the way in a town meeting, where resolutions, strongly condemning the treaty, were adopted and ordered to be transmitted to the President. He had made up his mind that the public interest required the confirmation of the treaty, and returned to the

Boston remonstrants a dispassionate answer to that effect. With this example from a portion of the country, where the strength of his administration was concentrated, it was not likely that the tone of opposition would be gentler in other parts of the Union. On the contrary, the vehemence with which the treaty was assailed daily gathered strength, and at length the barriers of deference toward the personal character of the President were wholly broken down. "The mission of Jay," says Chief Justice Marshall, in his "Life of Washington," "visibly affected the decorum which had been usually observed toward him, and the ratification of the treaty brought into open view feelings which had long been ill concealed. With equal virulence the military and political character of the President was attacked, and he was averred to be totally destitute of merit either as a soldier or a statesman. The calumnies with which he was assailed were not confined to his public conduct; even his qualities as a man were the subject of detraction. That he had violated the constitution in negotiating a treaty without the previous advice of the Senate, and in embracing within that treaty subjects belonging exclusively to the legislature, was openly maintained, for which an impeachment was publicly suggested; and that he had drawn from the treasury for his private use more than the salary annexed to his office, was unblushingly asserted!" Such was the frenzy of party; it afflicted Washington, but did not cause him to swerve a hair's breadth from his course.

An attempt was made, in the House of Representatives, to withhold the appropriations necessary to carry the treaty into effect. The party metaphysics of the day revelled in the plausible argument, which has since reappeared on similar occasions, that, as no money can be constitutionally drawn from the treasury without a specific appropriation, it was not competent for the President and Senate, as the treaty-making power, to pledge the faith of the country to the expenditure of money. It was forgotten, however, that a treaty is, by the same constitutional authority, the supreme law of the land, and, as such, binding on the conscience of the legislature. The extreme views of the opponents of the administration did not prevail, and the appropriations necessary to carry the treaty into effect passed the two Houses. It was on this subject that Mr. Fisher Ames, of Massachusetts, made the celebrated speech, which is still freshly remembered.

Among the other measures of the opposition, was the demand made by the

House of Representatives for the communication of the instructions under which the treaty was negotiated. In the modern usage of Congress, a call of this kind from either House is complied with as a matter of course; containing, as it always does, in important cases, a reservation that the communication can, in the President's opinion, be made without detriment to the public service. The practice of the government had not yet been established by usage, in reference to subjects of this kind. The demand for the communication of the instructions under which Mr. Jay had acted, was regarded, and justly, as a hostile movement against the administration, and the President refused to communicate the paper. He planted himself resolutely on the ground, that the treaty-making power was confided by the constitution to the President and Senate, and that it was not competent for the House of Representatives to require the communication of the instructions, which might have been given to the negotiators. The resolution, as originally moved, made an unqualified demand for the instructions and other papers connected with the treaty. Further reflection led the mover (Mr. Livingston) so far to modify the call, as to except from it papers, the communication of which might affect existing negotiations. A further amendment was moved by Mr. Madison, to except such papers "as it might be inconsistent with the interests of the United States at this time to disclose." But this wise and temperate suggestion, from the ablest and most sagacious member of the opposition, was rejected by a decisive vote of the House. Had it passed, it is probable that the President would have communicated the instructions, which, in the absence of that qualification, he resolutely withheld.

No transaction in the civil life of the President throws stronger light on the firmness of his character and his resolute adherence to principle. This has been shown by subsequent events more clearly than it was understood at the time. It was believed by the opponents of the administration, and that impression was no doubt shared to some extent by the public, that the instructions given to Mr. Jay might contain matters, which it would not be entirely convenient to the admin-istration, or the President as its head, to disclose. It was probably supposed by many persons, that Washington would have yielded to the request of the House of Representatives, had not some motive stronger than mere abstract principle prevented his doing so. It is the only instance, probably, in the history of the government, where a paper which could be laid before the public without inconvenience to the country or the administration, has, when asked for by either House of Congress, been withheld. Such, however, was indubitably the fact in this instance. The instructions in question remained for thirty years buried in the public archives, and undivulged. At length, in compliance with a call of the Senate of the United States in 1825, and in reference to the illegal captures of American vessels, made by the French cruisers prior to 1800, a mass of papers, filling a large octavo volume, was communicated to the Senate, and among them these once celebrated instructions. It was then found, by the few who took the trouble to examine them, as a matter of historical curiosity, that nothing could be more innocent; that they contained nothing which the most preju-

diced opponent could have tortured to
the discredit of the administration; and
that Washington had no motive whatever
for withholding them, but that of constitutional principle.

CHAPTER IX.

Insurrection in Pennsylvania suppressed — Washington's Interest in Lafayette — His Son received at Mount Vernon — Close of the Second Term of Office and Farewell Address — Denunciation of the spurious Letters — Retirement from the Presidency — Return to Mount Vernon — Rupture between the United States and France — Washington appointed Lieutenant-General — Anticipations of the Conflict — Downfall of the Directory, and Accommodation with France.

THE limits of this work do not admit of a detailed narrative of events, but we ought not to omit all mention of the firmness and resolution of Washington in calling into action the military force of the Union, to suppress almost the only formidable attempt to resist the laws, which has taken place since the adoption of the federal constitution. The tax levied on distilled spirits, in 1792, had been, from the first, unpopular in some portions of the country, and especially in western Pennsylvania. The newspapers teemed with inflammatory appeals to the people; the payment of the duty was in many cases refused; the tax-gatherers and other officers of the United States were insulted; meetings to oppose the law were held, and at length preparations made for organized forcible resistance. These proceedings extended over a period of nearly two years. Trusting to the return of reason on the part of the disaffected, no coercive measures, beyond the ordinary application of the law, were for a long time resorted to by the federal government. This lenity was, however, ascribed to fear, and led to daily increasing boldness on the part of the malecontents in western Pennsylvania, till, in 1794, it became manifest that more decisive measures must be adopted. The militia of the neighboring States of New Jersey, Maryland, and Virginia, were called out, in aid of the militia of Pennsylvania, to the amount in the whole of fifteen thousand troops. The President avowed the intention of taking the field in person, and repaired to the rendezvous of the troops at Cumberland and Bedford. These demonstrations produced the desired result; the disaffected perceived the madness of their course, and the insurrection subsided without a conflict.

President Washington's sympathies were warmly enlisted in favor of Lafayette, after it became necessary for him to abandon his army and give himself up to the Prussians. On his first arrival in this country, he had the good fortune, as we have seen, to gain the confidence of the Commander-in-chief, which he retained, by the uniform propriety of his

conduct, to the close of the war. There
is no stronger testimony to the solid
merit of the young French nobleman,
than his having played his difficult part,
military and political, to the entire satisfaction of his illustrious American chief.
The ties of personal attachment between
them were added to those of official confidence and respect. A friendly correspondence was kept up between Washington and Lafayette and his wife, after the
close of the Revolutionary War. The
hopeful interest taken by Washington in
the French revolution, in its early stages,
was, as has been stated, in some degree
inspired by regard for Lafayette, and by
confidence in his principles, of which he
had given such satisfactory proof in this
country. After his denunciation by the
Jacobins at Paris and his escape from
his army, Washington, having heard that
Madame Lafayette was in want abroad,

endeavored, through our ministers, to contribute to her relief, delicately seeking to make his donation assume the form of the repayment of a debt. After Lafayette, by a refinement of barbarous stupidity of which it would not be easy to find a parallel, had, though a fugitive from the guillotine in Paris, been thrown into a fortress in Austria, Washington addressed a letter in his favor to the Emperor of Germany. It received no answer; and Lafayette remained in the fortress of Olmütz, till, by a just retribution, his enlargement, which was refused to the respectful request of Washington, was extorted by the command of Napoleon. Sir Walter Scott, by a strange inadvertence, states, that Lafayette was given up on the 19th of December, 1795, in exchange for the Duchess d'Angoulême. His release was peremptorily demanded by Napoleon in the conferences at Leoben, which preceded the treaty of Campo Formio, and he was finally set at liberty on the 23d of September, 1797.

During his confinement, and while Madame Lafayette was imprisoned in Paris, (awaiting that fate which in one day had smitten her grandmother, the Duchess de Noailles, her mother, the Duchess d'Ayen, and her sister, the Countess de Noailles, but which she happily escaped by the downfall of Robespierre,) her son, George Washington Lafayette, just of age for the conscription, succeeded, through the friendly aid of the late Messrs. Thomas H. Perkins and Joseph Russell, of Boston, in making his escape to this country. He found a paternal welcome at Mount Vernon, where he lived, as a member of the family, for about three years, and returned to France on the liberation of his father.

During the residence of young Lafayette at Mount Vernon, the Duke of Orleans (afterwards King Louis Philippe) was also a visitor there with his brother; and tradition points to the border of the paper-hangings in one of the parlors, as having been cut out and prepared for pasting on the walls, by these young French exiles (in conjunction with the youthful members of the Washington family); happier perhaps, certainly freer from care, while so employed, than at any earlier or later period of their checkered and eventful lives.

At length the last year of General Washington's second quadriennial term of office arrived. Suggestions began to be made to him by his friends, looking to another reëlection, but nothing could now shake his purpose to retire; and he determined to put all doubt on that subject at rest, by a very formal announcement of his purpose. Having this immediate object in view, with parental interest in the present welfare of his countrymen, and provident forethought for the future, he determined to connect with it another object of still greater ulterior importance: a Farewell Address to his fellow-citizens, embodying his last counsels for their instruction and guidance. The steps taken by Washington for the preparation of this address, were marked with more than his usual circumspection and care. They have been the subject of some difference of opinion and discussion, at different times, in which it would exceed the limits of this work to engage. All the known facts of the case are brought together and set forth, with great acuteness and precision, by the Hon. Horace Binney, in the essay to which allusion has been made in the preface to these pages, entitled "An Inquiry into the Formation of Washington's Farewell Address."

It had been the intention of Washington, from an early period of his administration, to decline a reëlection at the close of the term of office for which he was chosen in 1789. Early in 1792, he considered the expediency of a farewell address in connection with the announcement of his purpose to retire. Among other confidential friends consulted by him at this time was Mr. Madison, with whom he communicated both orally at Philadelphia, and by letter after the recess of Congress. Mr. Madison, in reply to his letter, after earnestly dissuading the President from his purpose to retire, transmitted to him the draught of an address, which has been preserved. It is of no great length, and was evidently intended not to go far beyond the hints contained in the President's letter, either

in the choice or treatment of the topics.
Washington having been induced, by the
earnest and unanimous solicitation of his
friends, to consent to a reëlection, this
address was of course laid aside.

In the spring of 1796, and in the last
year of his second administration, having,
as we have seen, made up his mind irrev-
ocably to decline a re-nomination, Washington again took counsel on the subject
of a farewell address. In the progress of
the political divisions of the day, Mr.
Madison had ceased to be of the number
of his confidential advisers, and the President called upon Hamilton to aid him on
this occasion. Washington's first step was
to prepare himself a rough sketch of a
farewell address. It consisted of a few
preliminary sentences, introducing the
draught furnished by Mr. Madison in
1792, (to which, for particular reasons,
Washington adhered with some tenacity,)

and this was followed by the thoughts and sentiments, which he deemed most appropriate for such an address. As this paper was intended only to furnish materials, that portion of it which follows Madison's draught, and was composed by Washington himself, is a series of remarks and suggestions, not studiously arranged nor elaborated for promulgation. This paper was shown by Washington to Hamilton, at Philadelphia, in the spring of 1796, and the wish expressed that he would "re-dress" it. It was also suggested that, besides doing this, Hamilton, if he thought best, should "throw the whole into a new form," "predicated upon the sentiments contained" in Washington's draught.

This was accordingly done. Hamilton first prepared the address, thrown wholly into a "new form," and then digested in another paper, in connection with Mr.

Madison's short address, the thoughts and suggestions appended to it, as we have seen, in Washington's original draught. The President gave a decided preference to the " new form," and, after very careful revision by him, it was published on the 19th of September, 1796.

Of the documents and papers connected with this interesting production, there have been preserved, in addition to most if not all the correspondence between Washington and Hamilton, Washington's original rough draught of a farewell address and Hamilton's revision of it, (these two papers exist only in the copies taken by Mr. Sparks, the originals having disappeared,) and Hamilton's original draught of an address in the " new form." There is also preserved among Hamilton's papers " An abstract of Points to form an Address," which appears to have been drawn up by him as a guide, in preparing his original draught. Hamilton's original draught, as revised and corrected and adopted by Washington, has disappeared. The original manuscript of the Farewell Address, from which it was printed, is in existence, and it is wholly in the handwriting of Washington. It contains very many corrections, erasures, and interlineations, which are also all in Washington's handwriting. It was presented to the editor of the paper in which it was published, Claypoole, at his request, by Washington himself; and at Claypoole's decease it was purchased, for twenty-five hundred dollars, by James Lenox, Esq., of New York, who has caused a very carefully prepared edition of it to be privately printed, with all the variations accurately noted in the margin.

The above statement is believed to contain the material facts of the case, as far as they appear from the papers now in existence. The limits of these pages will not admit a more detailed investigation of the question of authorship, nor could it be made to advantage without a careful examination and comparison of the original papers in the case. From such an examination it will, we think, appear, that the Farewell Address, as drawn up by Hamilton and published by Washington to the people of the United States, commencing with the material portions of Mr. Madison's draught of 1792, presents, in a more developed form, the various ideas contained in Washington's original draught, and treats, in argumentative connection, the topics therein more aphoristically propounded; the whole combined with original suggestions of a kindred type from Hamilton's own pen. Great skill is evinced by him in interweaving, in its proper place, every suggestion contained in Washington's draught, (with a

single exception); nor is there believed to
be anything superadded by Hamilton, of
which the germ at least cannot be found
in Washington's draught, in his multifari-
ous correspondence, or in other produc-
tions unquestionably from his pen.

A single topic contained in Washington's draught was excluded, with his full
consent and approbation, from the published address. The passage in question
consisted of suggestions of a personal
character, — an indignant allusion to the
efforts made by "some of the gazettes of
the United States," by misrepresentations
and falsehoods, "to wound his reputation
and feelings," and "to weaken if not entirely destroy the confidence" reposed in
him by the country; a proud assertion
of the uprightness of his intentions; a
touching demand of respect for "the gray
hairs of a man" who had passed the
prime of his life in the service of the

country, that he may "be suffered to pass quietly to his grave;" with a concluding observation that his fortune had not been improved by the emoluments of office. These ideas, rather more carefully digested than any other portion of Washington's original draught, are, in the published address, omitted almost wholly, and this with the distinct approbation of Washington. It appears to have been thought that, in a paper calculated to descend to posterity, allusions to temporary causes of irritation had better be suppressed. From this opinion we are compelled, with great diffidence, to dissent. We are under the impression that, though this part of Washington's draught, like the rest of it, (but less than the other portions,) was "in a rough state," the substance of it, with some softening of the language, which was never intended for publication, might have been retained. The opponents of Washington were not conciliated by its absence, and posterity has lost a lesson on the license and ferocity of party defamation, nearly as important as any contained in the address. It reflects new lustre on the modesty of Washington, that, in a matter personal to himself, he deferred to the judgment of his trusted friend; but this judgment, in the present case, we conceive to have been erroneous.

It may finally be observed that Washington, with reference to this address, as to every act in life, aimed, with the entire sacrifice of self, to accomplish the desired good. He was accustomed, as a military chieftain, to employ daily the pens of active and intelligent secretaries, in communicating his plans, transmitting his commands, and generally carrying on his correspondence, without the thought that they were any the less the dictates of his own mind and judgment, because conveyed in the words of another. This habit he carried with him to the presidency, freely putting in requisition the aid of such official advisers and personal friends as in his opinion would best enable him to perform the duty of the day. In doing this, he retained and exercised an independent judgment, and he adopted nothing furnished to him by others, which did not, after rigid scrutiny, stand the test of his own marvellous discernment and unerring wisdom.

The vice-president, Mr. John Adams, was chosen his successor by a majority so slender * as to show that the country was now divided into two parties nearly equal. The tone of the public journals and the debates in Congress displayed an intensity of party feeling usually found under similar circumstances. Twelve mem-

* For John Adams, 71; for Thomas Jefferson, 68.

bers of the House of Representatives voted against the response of the House to the President's address to Congress at the opening of the last session, and a member from Virginia allowed himself to say, "that he did not regret the President's retirement." On the 3d of March, the last day of his administration, he gave a farewell dinner to the foreign ministers, the president and vice-president elect, and other distinguished persons of both sexes. Much hilarity prevailed; till, toward the close of the entertainment, filling his glass, he said to the company, with a gracious smile, "Ladies and gentlemen, this is the last time I shall drink your health as a public man. I do it with sincerity, wishing you all possible happiness." Bishop White, in relating this anecdote, adds that there was an end of all gayety; and that having directed his eye accidentally to Lady Liston, the wife of the British minister, he perceived the tears running down her cheeks. The next day General Washington attended the inauguration of President Adams, and received on that occasion the most striking tokens of the public respect and veneration. The crowd followed him with acclamations, from the chamber of the House of Representatives, where the inaugural ceremonies of his successor were performed, to his own door. "There turning round, his countenance assumed a grave and almost melancholy expression, his eyes were bathed in tears, his emotions were too great for utterance, and only by his gestures could he indicate his thanks and convey his farewell blessing."* Similar demonstrations of respect were repeated at a splendid enter-

* President W. A. Duer's recollections, in Irving's *Washington*, vol. v. p. 271.

tainment given to him in the evening by the citizens of Philadelphia.

The last official letter of General Washington, as President of the United States, was addressed to the secretary of state, for the purpose of placing on record a formal denunciation of the forgeries, to which allusion has been already made. This letter, after denying the truth of the facts which were alleged for the sake of giving a show of probability to this wretched fabrication, adds, with touching pathos, "As I cannot know how soon a more serious event may succeed to that which will this day take place, I have thought it a duty which I owed to myself, to my country, and to truth, now to detail the circumstances above recited; and to add my solemn declaration that the letters herein described are a base forgery, and that I never saw or heard of them till they appeared in print."

Washington left Philadelphia about the 11th or 12th of March, 1797, accompanied by Mrs. Washington, Miss Custis, and George Washington Lafayette and his tutor, and returned to Mount Vernon by the way of Baltimore, followed by the blessings of the people.

Here it was his fondly cherished wish and hope to pass the remainder of his days in tranquil retirement. He was sixty-five years of age, a few days before he retired from the presidency, and, as has been already mentioned, he did not consider himself as of a long-lived family. He had taken a definitive leave of political life; he was fond of agricultural pursuits; and his private affairs, much neglected during the eight years of his presidency, as they had also been while he was in the military service of the country, imperatively demanded his attention. In addition to this, the state of parties was such as to dispose him more than ever to stand aloof. Extreme opinions, tending in opposite directions, more than ever divided the country; and the voice of moderation, always scorned by zealots, was, even if uttered by Washington, less likely than ever to be heard.

But his hopes of unmolested retirement, however ardently cherished, were doomed to be disappointed. The course pursued by the French Directory was such as to exhaust the patience alike of the government and people of the United States. From the first arrival of M. Genet in this country, in 1793, although his successor did not come quite up to the standard of his indecorum, our diplomatic relations with France had been of the most unsatisfactory kind. Our neutrality in the war raging in Europe was, or was pretended to be, taken in ill part, and the negotiation of Jay's treaty gave new cause of offence. While the French ministers in this country scarcely kept within the bounds of civility toward the federal government, our ministers to France were either not received, or received to be insulted, and our commerce was surrendered a hopeless prey to the public cruisers and the privateers of the Republic.

It was necessary that outrages like these, of which the injury was great, and the shame worse than the injury, should at length have an end. The despatches of our envoys to France, detailing the affronts which had been put upon them and their country, were laid before Congress; and a just resentment was kindled in that body and throughout the Union. A suitable addition was voted to the naval and military force of the United States, and active preparations commenced for the impending conflict. With the first serious alarm of an approaching struggle all eyes were turned toward Washington, as the necessary leader of the armies of the country. No other person was thought of for the chief command. Washington was early prepared for the call which could not fail to be made upon him, by the letters of his confidential friends; and though sagaciously predicting that the French Directory would not have the madness to push matters to a war, he avowed his purpose to obey the call of the country. After alluding to his occupations at Mount Vernon, he adds, in writing to Hamilton, "If a crisis should arrive when a sense of duty or a call from my country should become so imperious as to leave me no choice, I should prepare for relinquishment, and go with as much reluctance from my present peaceful abode, as I should go to the tomb of my ancestors."

The unwelcome necessity presented itself. Toward the close of June, 1798, letters were addressed to General Washington, both by the president and the secretary of war, tendering to him informally the command of the army about to be organized. His replies were in unison with the sentiment just quoted, though filled with expressions of distress at the thoughts of leaving his retirement. Some delay took place in the transmission of the letters of the president and the secretary to Mount Vernon, and before the answers to them could be received at the seat of government, Washington had been nominated to the Senate by President Adams, as Commander-in-chief of the armies of the United States, with the rank of lieutenant-general; a title never conferred in any other instance in the United States, before or since, except in that of General Scott, on whom it was justly bestowed a few years since by Congress.

General Washington accepted the commission, stipulating only that he should not take the field till the army was in a situation to need his presence, or the country was actually invaded. The President, however, in the letter communicating his appointment, had declared that he stood in urgent need of his advice and assistance, and indeed "of his conduct and direction of the war;" and Washington engaged in the organization of the army with the spirit and energy of earlier days. Difficulties and embarrassments of no ordinary kind presented themselves; but the experience of two wars and two civil administrations had sufficiently taught him that these are, unhappily, at all times, the conditions of the public service. It may be stated, in general terms, that the main difficulties which attend the administration of a government, in peace or in war, spring not so much from the necessary and intrinsic conditions of the public service, as from the selfishness and the passions of individuals, and the madness of parties.

There is a suggestion in a long and very interesting letter to the secretary of war, of the 4th of July, 1799, written in reply to the overtures above alluded to, which shows that the newly appointed Commander-in-chief was fully aware of the tremendous risks to which his military reputation might be exposed. He had evidently reflected on the possibility that he might be brought into actual conflict with the youthful French chieftain, who had already filled the world with the rumor of his military genius, in those campaigns of 1796 and 1797, to which Europe had seen no parallel since the days of Julius Cæsar. After some modest allusions to his advancing years, Washington, in the letter referred to, says, " I express these ideas not from affectation, for I despise everything that carries that appearance, but from the belief, that as it is the fashion of the present day, set or adopted by the French, (with whom we are to contend,) and with great and astonishing success too, to appoint *generals of juvenile years* to lead their armies, it might not be impossible that similar ideas and wishes might pervade the minds of our citizens." It was his often repeated sentiment, that if the French attempted to gain a foothold in the country they must not be permitted to land; and his reference to their youthful commanders shows that he must have contemplated the probability that, in the event of a war, he should be brought in direct collision with the youngest and most successful of them, — the hero of

Arcole and Lodi. But the "man of destiny" had been led by his star in another direction, and the man of Providence was not called to meet him in the field. Four days before the letter of Washington, just cited, was written, Napoleon had landed at Alexandria. The Directory saw, before it was too late, the madness of their proceedings, and showed a willingness to retrace their steps, by an intimation that another mission from the United States would be honorably received. They might with propriety have been required by this government to take the initiative in the work of peace, and to send their own envoys to this country. But the United States were then a feeble power, and the administration was harassed by dissensions among its political friends, and by a formidable opposition. President Adams probably adopted the more prudent course in closing with the overture of the Directory. In the mean time the wheel of fortune was revolving: the bloody game of Egypt had been played out; Napoleon had returned to France; the Directory had sunk before him; and his brother Joseph, on the 30th of September, 1800, concluded with Messrs. Ellsworth, Davy, and Murray, a treaty of peace.

CHAPTER X.

Sudden Attack of Illness in December, 1799 — Rapid Progress and Fatal Termination of the Disease — Public Mourning — Emancipation of his Slaves by Will — Mount Vernon — Personal Appearance and Habits — Religious Opinions — General Views of his Character — Testimony of Lord Erskine, of Mr. Fox, of Lord Brougham, of Fontanes, and of Guizot — His Military Character — Natural Temperament — Genius for the Conduct of Affairs — Final Estimate.

THE conclusion of a treaty of peace with France was a fulfilment of his anticipations, which Washington did not live to witness. His illustrious life was drawing unexpectedly to a close. December, 1799, found him apparently in unusual health. His favorite nephew Lewis, writing of him as he appeared to himself and a friend at that time, says, " The clear and healthy flush on his cheek and his sprightly manner brought the remark from both of us, that we had never seen the General look so well. I have sometimes thought him decidedly the handsomest man I ever saw." On the 10th of December, 1799, he completed the draught of an elaborate plan for the management of his plantations, laying down the rotation of the crops, for a succession of years in advance. The morning of that day was clear and calm, but the afternoon was lowering. The next, the 11th of December, was a blustering, rainy day; and at night, says the diary, " there was a large circle round the moon."

The morning of the 12th was overcast. Washington's last letter was written that morning. It was to Hamilton, and principally on the subject of a military academy. At ten o'clock he rode out as usual over his farms. " About one o'clock," he remarks in his diary, " it began to snow, soon after to hail, and then turned to a settled, cold rain." He was, however, protected by an outside coat, and remained in the saddle five hours.

On franking the letters brought to him for that purpose by his secretary, he said the weather was too bad to send a servant to the post-office, which was at Alexandria, nine miles off. His secretary, Mr. Lear, from whose narration these minute details are derived, perceiving that snow was clinging to his hair behind, expressed his fears that his neck must be wet. He said it was not, that his greatcoat had kept him dry. He went to dinner, which had been kept waiting for him, without changing his dress, and in the evening appeared as well as usual.

There were three inches of snow on

the ground on the morning of Friday, the 13th, and it continued to fall. In consequence of this state of the weather, and of a sore throat of which he complained, evidently the result of his exposure the day before, Washington omitted his usual morning ride around his plantations. It cleared up, however, in the afternoon, and he went out to mark some trees, which were to be cut down for the improvement of the grounds, between the river and the house. He had a hoarseness upon him at this time, which increased in the evening, but he made light of it. This was the last time that he left his house.

The newspapers were brought from the post-office in the evening, and he passed it in the parlor reading them. At nine o'clock Mrs. Washington went up to the room of her grand-daughter, Mrs. Lewis, (who was confined,) leaving the General and Mr. Lear together. He was very cheerful, and when he found anything of interest read it aloud, as well as his hoarseness would permit. He requested Mr. Lear to read aloud the debates in the Virginia Assembly on the election of senator and governor; and discovered some feeling at the remarks of Mr. Madison respecting Mr. Monroe. When he retired for the night, Mr. Lear advised him to take something for his cold. He answered, " No, you know I never take anything for a cold; let it go as it came." These were the last words, hopeful of health, which passed his lips.

Saturday, the 14th, was the last day of his life; it was long and full of suffering. Between two and three o'clock in the morning, he awoke Mrs. Washington, telling her he had had an ague-fit, and was very unwell. He could then scarcely speak, and breathed with difficulty. Thoughtful of others even in this emergency, he would not allow her to get up to call a servant, for fear of her taking cold. At daybreak, Caroline the servant came to make a fire, and was sent by her mistress to call Mr. Lear. Hastening to the General's chamber, Mr. Lear found him breathing with difficulty, and hardly able to articulate. He desired that his friend and physician, Dr. Craik, who lived in Alexandria, should be sent for, and that in the mean time Mr. Rawlins, one of the overseers, should bleed him.

A soothing mixture was prepared for his throat, but he was unable to swallow the smallest quantity. The effort to do so caused distress, — almost suffocation. Rawlins came soon after sunrise, and prepared to bleed him. When the arm was ready, Washington, perceiving that he was agitated, said, as plainly as he could,

"Don't be afraid;" and when the vein was opened, observed, "The orifice is not large enough." The blood flowed pretty freely; but Mrs. Washington, fearful that bloodletting might not be proper, begged that much should not be taken. When Mr. Lear, however, was about to untie the ligature, the General raised his hand to prevent it, saying, "More, more." Mrs. Washington being still anxious lest he should suffer by the loss of blood, about half a pint only was taken. His throat was now bathed with *sal volatile*, and his feet placed in warm water; but without affording any relief. When the hand of the attendant was gently applied to his throat, he said, "It is very sore." About eight o'clock he rose and was dressed; — but he found no relief from the change of position, and at ten returned to his bed.

The alarm rapidly increasing, a physician was sent for from Port Tobacco, on the other side of the river; but between eight and nine o'clock Dr. Craik arrived. He immediately applied a blister to the throat, took more blood, and had a gargle prepared, which, however, the patient was wholly unable to use. Other remedial applications were attempted, but without effect. At eleven o'clock a third physician was sent for; and in the mean time the General was again bled.. No benefit resulted from this treatment, and he remained unable to swallow.

About three o'clock Drs. Dick and Brown arrived; and, after consultation, the sufferer was for the fourth time bled. The blood came thick and slow, but its loss produced no faintness. He was now able to swallow a little, and active medicines were administered, but without beneficial effect.

About half-past four o'clock Mrs. Washington was called to his bedside, and he requested her to go to his room and bring from his desk two wills, which she did. He looked at them, handed her one to burn as useless, and gave the other into her possession.

After this, Mr. Lear returned to his bedside and took his hand. "I find," said the General, "I am going. My breath cannot last long. I believed from the first that the disorder would prove fatal. Do you arrange and record all my late military letters and papers. Arrange my accounts and settle my books, and let Mr. Rawlins finish recording my other letters, which he has begun." He then asked Mr. Lear if he recollected anything which it was essential for him to do, as he had but a very short time to continue with them. Mr. Lear expressed the hope that he was not so near his end. He observed, with a smile, that he certainly was, and that, as it was the debt which we must all pay, he looked to it with perfect resignation.

In the course of the afternoon he was helped up, and after sitting about half an hour, desired to be undressed again, and put to bed. Perceiving his servant Christopher, who had been in attendance most of the day, to be standing, he thoughtfully told him to be seated. In the course of the afternoon, he suffered great pain from the difficulty of breathing, and desired frequently to change his position in bed. On these occasions his secretary lay by his side, in order to turn him with as much ease as possible. He was touched with these attentions, and said, "I am afraid I shall fatigue you too much; it is a debt we must pay to each other, and I hope, when you want aid of this kind, you will find it."

About five o'clock in the afternoon, Dr.

Craik came again into the room, and upon his going to the bedside the General said to him, "Doctor, I die hard, but I am not afraid to go. I believed from my first attack, that I should not survive it. My breath cannot last long." Dr. Craik, his companion on the field of battle and his friend through life, perceiving that the last hour was near, pressed the hand of Washington, but could not speak, and left the bedside in speechless grief.

Between five and six, the three physicians approached his bedside. Dr. Craik asking if he could sit up in bed, he held out his hand and was raised up. He then said to the physicians, "I feel myself going; I thank you for your attentions; but I pray you to take no more trouble about me. Let me go off quietly; I cannot last long." He lay down again; restless and suffering, but without complaining, frequently asking what hour it was.

About eight o'clock the physicians again came into the room, and applied blisters and cataplasms to the legs. At ten o'clock he made several attempts to speak to Mr. Lear, but for some time without success. At length he said, "I am just going; have me decently buried; and do not let my body be put into the vault, till three days 'after I am dead." Mr. Lear, unable to speak, bowed assent. He then spoke again and said, "Do you understand me?" Mr. Lear replied that he did; and Washington said, "It is well."

These were the last words which he uttered. Between ten and eleven o'clock, and about ten minutes before he died, his breathing became easier. He lay quietly, withdrew his hand from Mr. Lear's, and felt his own pulse. At this moment his countenance changed, his hand fell from his wrist, and he expired without a struggle. Mrs. Washington, who was seated at the foot of the bed, said in a collected voice, "Is he gone?" A signal from Mr. Lear gave the answer. "It is well," she said; "all is now over; I shall soon follow him; I have no more trials to pass through."

The disease of which General Washington died was what is now technically called "acute laryngitis," a disease of very rare occurrence, and at that time not discriminated from other inflammatory diseases of the throat. The mournful interest which attaches to the closing scenes of this illustrious career, has led the author of these pages to solicit from the venerable Dr. James Jackson, of Boston, a professional memoir on the subject of his disease and the manner in which it was treated by his attendant physicians.* "During his whole illness," says Mr. Lear, in the memorandum from which the foregoing account is taken almost *verbatim*, "he spoke but seldom, and with great difficulty and distress; and in so low and broken a voice, as at times hardly to be understood. His patience, fortitude, and resignation never forsook him for a moment. In all his distress he uttered not a sigh nor a complaint; always endeavoring, from a sense of duty, as it appeared, to take what was offered to him, and to do as he was desired by his physician."

On the 18th of December, followed by the sorrowing members of his family, by his friends, and neighbors, his mortal remains were deposited in the family vault at Mount Vernon, where they still rest. In consequence of the suddenness of the event, the news of his illness and

* See Appendix, No. I.

of his death went out at once to the country; and fell like the tidings of a domestic sorrow upon the hearts of the people. Appropriate resolutions, drawn by General Lee, one of the members from Virginia, were, in his absence, moved by his colleague, Mr. John Marshall, afterwards chief justice of the United States, expressive of the public sorrow at the loss of him, who was "first in war, first in peace, and first in the hearts of his fellow-citizens." The tributes of respect paid to his memory by Congress were repeated by the state legislatures, the courts, the municipal bodies, the seats of learning, and the associations of every description throughout the Union; and all the people mourned.

We have already seen that a few hours before his death Washington sent to his study for two wills, which, when brought, were handed by him to Mrs. Washington, one to be destroyed, and the other preserved by her. As he had kept them both to the close of his life, it may be supposed that, in conformity with his strictly methodical business habits, the two wills had been prepared by him, to meet respectively the contingencies of surviving his wife or dying before her. Although, as he frequently observes in his correspondence, his affairs had greatly suffered by his long absences from home, he left a large estate. He inherited a small property from his father; his elder brother bequeathed to him the estate of Mount Vernon; he received a large accession of wealth with his wife; and he made extensive purchases of unimproved lands, not only in Virginia but in several other states, some of which probably rose in value. A schedule appended to his will, of that part of his property which was to be sold for distribution among his general heirs, amounts, as estimated by him, to something more than half a million of dollars. The larger part of his estate was specifically bequeathed, and must have more than equalled this amount. President Adams the elder, writing to a friend in Massachusetts, at the time of Washington's election as Commander-in-chief, in 1775, speaks of him as "a gentleman of one of the finest fortunes upon the continent." It is probable that many of the unimproved lands, though possessing a speculative value, were unproductive; and of stocks and other property yielding a fixed income the amount appears to have been small.

By the third *item* of the will, which was made about six months before his death, General Washington provided that, upon the decease of his wife, all the slaves held by him in his own right should receive their freedom. "To emancipate them during her life," the will proceeds, "would, though earnestly wished by me, be attended with such insuperable difficulties, on account of their intermixture by marriage with the dower negroes, as to excite the most painful sensations, if not disagreeable consequences, to the latter, while both descriptions are in the occupancy of the same proprietor; it not being in my power, under the tenure by which the dower negroes are held, to manumit them." For those emancipated, who from old age or bodily infirmity should be unable to support themselves, the will directs that a comfortable provision of food and clothing while they lived should be made by his heirs. Those who were too young to support themselves, and who had no parents able or willing to support them, were to be bound by the court till they were twenty-five years of age; were to be taught to read and write by the masters to whom they were bound; and brought up to some useful occupation. The will expressly forbids the sale or transportation out of Virginia of any slave of whom he might die possessed, under any pretence whatsoever; and it enforces the general intentions of the testator in the following stringent terms: "And I do moreover most pointedly and most solemnly enjoin upon my executors . . to see that this clause respecting slaves and every part thereof be religiously fulfilled at the epoch at which it is directed to take place, without evasion, neglect, or delay, after the crops which may then be on the ground are harvested, particularly as it respects the aged and infirm; seeing that a regular and permanent fund be established for their support, as long as there are subjects requiring it; not trusting to the uncertain provision to be made by individuals."

For his favorite servant Billy, who attended him throughout the revolutionary war, a special provision was made in the following terms, and with characteristic precision: —

"To my mulatto man William, calling himself William Lee, I give immediate freedom, or, if he should prefer it, (on account of the accidents which have befallen him, and which have rendered him incapable of walking, or of any active employment,) to remain in the situation he now is, it shall be optional in him to do so; in either case, however, I allow him an annuity of thirty dollars, during his natural life, which shall be independent of the victuals and clothes he has been accustomed to receive, if he chooses the last alternative; but in full with his freedom, if he prefers the first; and this

I give him as a testimony of my sense of his attachment to me, and for his faithful services during the revolutionary war."

The estate of Mount Vernon was bequeathed to his nephew, Bushrod Washington, (the son of the General's younger and favorite brother, John A. Washington,) afterwards one of the associate justices of the supreme court of the United States. This bequest was made, in the words of the testator, "partly in consideration of an intimation to his deceased father, while we were bachelors, and he had kindly undertaken to superintend my estate during my military services in the former war between Great Britain and France, that, if I should fall therein, Mount Vernon, then less extensive in domain than at present, should become his property." On the decease of Mr. Justice Washington without children, it came into the possession of a nephew, who bequeathed it to his widow. Her son, John A. Washington, is the present incumbent. Two years since, a contract was entered into between Mr. John A. Washington and "The Ladies' Mount Vernon Association of the Union," for the purchase of two hundred acres of the estate, including the mansion-house and the tomb, for two hundred thousand dollars. The greater part of the stipulated purchase-money has been already paid.

We have, in the foregoing memoir, aimed to present the reader with a comprehensive though necessarily greatly condensed sketch of the principal events of the life of Washington, as the best means of conveying an adequate impression of his character. As his active life covers very nearly half a century of the most important period in the history of the Anglo-American colonies and of the United States, and as he was himself intimately associated with the events of greatest consequence while he was on the stage, it was manifestly necessary to pass rapidly over the ground. Much has of necessity been omitted, and much superficially narrated. The works of the standard authors mentioned in the preface have furnished most of the materials of the foregoing narrative; and their own words have been sometimes borrowed. The reader will perhaps wish that this had been done oftener.

General Washington's personal appearance was in harmony with his character; it was a model of manly strength and beauty. He was about six feet two inches in height, and his person well-proportioned,— in the earlier part of life rather spare, and never too stout for active and graceful movement. The complexion inclined to the florid; the eyes were blue and remarkably far apart; a profusion of brown hair was drawn back from the forehead, highly powdered according to the fashion of the day, and gathered in a bag behind. He was scrupulously neat in his dress, and while in camp, though he habitually left his tent at sunrise, he was usually dressed for the day. His strength of arm, and his skill and grace as a horseman, have been already mentioned. His power of endurance was great, and there were occasions, as at the retreat from Long Island and the battle of Princeton, when he was scarcely out of his saddle for two days. Punctilious in his observance of the courtesies of society as practised in his day, he was accustomed, down to the period of his inauguration as President, at the balls given in his honor, to take part in a minuet or country-dance. His diary uniformly records, sometimes with amusing exactness, the precise number of ladies present at the assemblies, at which he was received on his tours through the Union. His general manner in large societies, though eminently courteous, was marked by a certain military reserve. In smaller companies he was easy and affable, but not talkative. He was frequently cheered into gayety, at his fireside, by the contagious merriment of the young and happy, but often relapsed into a thoughtful mood, moving his lips, but uttering no audible sound.

Washington's religious impressions were in harmony with the rest of his character,—deep, rational, and practical. On this topic, our remaining space admits of little more than a reference to the interesting article on this subject in the fourth section of the appendix to Mr. Sparks's twelfth volume. Washington was brought up in the Episcopal communion, and was a member of the vestry of two churches. He was at all times a regular attendant on public worship, and an occasional partaker of the communion; and is believed habitually to have begun the day with the reading of the Scriptures and prayer in his closet. His private correspondence, his general orders, and his public acts of all kinds contain devout recognitions of a divine Providence in the government of the world, and his whole life bears witness to the influence of a prevailing sense of religious responsibility. In his last moments he breathed a truly pious spirit of resignation. In his own affecting words, he died "hard," but he was "not afraid to go." Though prevented, by the rapid progress of his disease, and the almost total obstruction of the vocal organs, from expressing his feelings, he manifested to the last the submission of a sincere Christian to the will of the great Disposer.

Posterity will not be left without a faithful representation of his person. The statue by Houdon in the capitol at Richmond, modelled at the age of fifty-three, is the accepted embodiment of his countenance and form, and has been followed substantially by all his successors, in several monumental works of distinguished merit. A series of portraits by able artists, from the age of thirty-eight onwards, delineate him under all the modifications of feature and person gradually induced by the advance of years.*

In the final contemplation of his character, we shall not hesitate to pronounce

---

* An instructive enumeration and description of the portraits of Washington, preceded by an extremely judicious essay on his character, will be found in a monograph entitled *Character and Portraits of Washington*, by Henry T. Tuckerman, Esq.

Washington, of all men that have ever lived, THE GREATEST OF GOOD MEN AND THE BEST OF GREAT MEN. Nor let this judgment be attributed to national partiality. In the year 1797, Mr. Rufus King, then the American minister in London, wrote to General Hamilton, "No one, who has not been in England, can have a just idea of the admiration expressed among all parties for General Washington. It is a common observation, that he is not only the most illustrious, but the most meritorious character that has yet appeared." Lord Erskine, in writing to Washington about the same time, says, "You are the only human being for whom I ever felt an awful reverence." Mr. Charles James Fox remarks of him, that "A character of virtues, so happily tempered by one another and so wholly unalloyed by any vices, as that of Washington, is hardly to be found on the pages of history." Lord

Brougham, in his brilliant comparative sketch of Napoleon and Washington, after a glowing picture of the virtues and vices of the great modern conqueror, exclaims, "How grateful the relief, which the friend of mankind, the lover of virtue, experiences, when, turning from the contemplation of such a character, his eye rests upon the greatest man of our own or of any age, the only one upon whom an epithet, so thoughtlessly lavished by men, may be innocently and justly bestowed!" Nor are these testimonies confined to Englishmen, in whom they might be supposed to be inspired, in some degree, by Anglo-Saxon sympathy. When the news of his death reached France, Fontanes, by direction of Napoleon, delivered an eloquent eulogium, in which he declared him to be "a character worthy the best days of antiquity." M. Guizot, a far higher authority, in his admirable essay on the character of Washington, pronounces that "Of all great men he was the most virtuous and the most fortunate."

The comparison of Napoleon and Washington suggests a remark on the military character of the latter, who is frequently disparaged in contrast with the great chieftains of ancient and modern times. But no comparison can be instituted to any valuable purpose between individuals, which does not extend to the countries and periods in which they lived and to the means at their command. When these circumstances are taken into the account, Washington, as a chieftain, I am inclined to think, will sustain the comparison with any other of ancient or modern time. A recent judicious French writer (M. Edouard Laboulaye), though greatly admiring the character of Washington, denies him the brilliant military genius of Julius Cæsar. It is, to say the least, as certain that Julius Cæsar, remaining in other respects what he was, could not have conducted the American Revolution to a successful issue, as that Washington could not have subdued Gaul, thrown an army into Great Britain, or gained the battle of Pharsalia. No one has ever denied to Washington the possession of the highest degree of physical and moral courage; no one has ever accused him of missing an opportunity to strike a bold blow; no one has pointed out a want of vigor in the moment of action, or of forethought in the plans of his campaigns; in short, no one has alleged a fact, from which it can be made even probable that Napoleon or Cæsar, working with his means and on his field of action, could have wrought out greater or better results than he did, or that, if he had been placed on a field of action and with a command of means like theirs, he would have shown himself unequal to the position.

There is, in this respect, a great mistake on the subject of Washington's temperament, which was naturally sanguine. Traditionary accounts, which must, however, be received with great caution as far as particular anecdotes are concerned, authorize the belief that, in early life at least, he habitually waged a strenuous war fare with his own ardent temper. At all events, while he was placed in circumstances, in both his wars, which forced upon him the Fabian policy, there were occasions, as we have seen in the narration, when he seized the opportunity of making what, if it had failed, would have been called a rash movement. This showed him the possessor of an expansive capacity; conforming patiently to straits, and keeping good heart in adversity, but ready at a moment of change to move with vigor and power. When we add to this an unquestioned fondness for the military profession, who can doubt that, if he had been trained in the great wars of Europe, he would have proved himself equal to their severest tests? It is a remarkable fact, that from his youth upward he evinced military capacity beyond that of all the trained and . experienced officers, with whom he was associated or brought in conflict. The neglect of his advice in 1755 cost the veteran Braddock his army and his life, and threw the valley of the Ohio into the power of the French; and all the skill and energy visible in the operations of General Forbes by which it was recovered in 1758, were infused into them by Washington.

Akin to the argument against his military capacity, is the question whether, generally speaking, Washington was a man of genius,—a question not to be answered till that word is explained. Dr. Johnson calls it, "that power which constitutes a poet," and in that acceptation Washington certainly was not endowed with it. As little did he possess the genius of the orator, the man of letters, the sculptor, the painter, the musician. The term is so habitually, not to say exclusively, appropriated to that native power which enables men to excel in science, literature, and the fine arts, that those who are destitute of it in these departments are often declared to want it altogether. But there is a genius of political and military skill; of social influence, of personal ascendency, of government;— a genius for practical utility; a moral genius of true heroism, of unselfish patriotism, and of stern public integrity, which is as strongly marked an endow-

ment as those gifts of intellect, imagina-
tion, and taste, which constitute the poet
or the artist. Without adopting Virgil's
magnificent but scornful contrast between
scientific and literary skill, on the one
hand, and those masterful arts on the
other, by which victories are gained and
nations are governed, we must still admit, that the chieftain who, in spite of
obstacles the most formidable, and vicissi-
tudes the most distressing, conducts great
wars to successful issues, — that the statesman who harmonizes angry parties in
peace, skilfully moderates the counsels
of constituent assemblies, and, without the
resources of rhetoric but by influence
mightier than authority, secures the formation and organization of governments,
and in their administration establishes
the model of official conduct for all following time, is endowed with a divine
principle of thought and action, as dis-

tinct in its kind as that of Demosthenes
or Milton. It is the genius of a consummate manhood. Analysis may describe its manifestations in either case,
but cannot define the ulterior principle.
It is a final element of character. We
may speak of prudence, punctuality, and
self-control, of bravery and disinterested-
ness, as we speak of an eye for color
and a perception of the graceful in the
painter, a sensibility to the sublime, the
pathetic, and the beautiful in discourse;
but behind and above all these there
must be a creative and animating principle; at least as much in character as in
intellect or art. The qualities which per-
tain to genius are not the whole of
genius in the one case any more than
the other. The arteries, the lungs, and
the nerves are essential to life, but they
are not life itself,—that higher something,
which puts all the organic functions of

the frame in motion. In the possession of that mysterious quality of character, manifested in a long life of unambitious service, which, called by whatever name, inspires the confidence, commands the respect, and wins the affection of contemporaries, and grows upon the admiration of successive generations, forming a standard to which the merit of other men is referred, and a living proof that pure patriotism is not a delusion, nor virtue an empty name, no one of the sons of men has equalled GEORGE WASHINGTON.

APPENDIX.

No. I.

MEMOIR ON THE LAST SICKNESS OF GENERAL WASH-
INGTON AND ITS TREATMENT BY THE ATTENDANT
PHYSICIANS. BY JAMES JACKSON, M. D.

THE death of General Washington took place unexpectedly after an illness of less than forty-eight hours. He was
in his sixty-eighth year, but had not begun to show much of
the infirmities of age. Under the exposures of the active
period of his life, and again shortly after he had engaged in
the heavy cares and responsibilities of office in 1789, he had
undergone severe acute diseases; but it does not appear that
he had been suffering under any wearing or wasting chronic
malady. His faithful biographer, Mr. Sparks, says of him,
that " Since his retirement from the presidency, his health
had been remarkably good; and although age had not come
without its infirmities, yet he was able to endure fatigue, and
make exertions of body and mind with scarcely less ease and
activity than he had done in the prime of his strength." *
Such being the case, the circumstances of his short disease,
its character viewed scientifically, and the propriety of the
treatment adopted by his physicians, have all been ascer-

* Sparks's *Life of Washington*, p. 528.

tained and discussed; and the remedies employed have been spoken of by some persons in terms of strong reprobation.

We derive the only original account of his disease from a statement made out by Colonel Lear within twenty-four hours after his decease, with an attestation to the correctness of this account made at the time, "so far as he could recollect," by his excellent friend and physician, Dr. Craik. This account has the appearance of accuracy and fidelity. It is consistent with itself, and accords with what is now known to belong to the disease which cut short the days of this great man.

On the 12th of December, 1799, he was abroad on his farms, on horseback, from 10 o'clock A. M. to 3 P. M.; and "soon after he went out the weather became very bad, rain, hail, and snow falling alternately, with a cold wind." To the watchful eyes of his family there were no appearances of disease, though they looked for them, until the next day. He then complained of a sore throat, and it became evident that he had taken cold; "he had a hoarseness, which increased in the evening; but he made light of it." So far from feeling anything like serious illness on this 13th of December, he seems to have been kept from "riding out, as usual," only by a snow-storm. In the afternoon he went out of the house to look after some work, which was not of an urgent character. He passed his evening as usual, and did not seem to be aware that his cold was uncommonly severe. When Colonel Lear proposed at bedtime that he should take "something to remove his cold," he answered, "No, you know I never take anything for a cold; let it go as it came."

It was in this night that his sickness arrested his attention. He was taken with an ague, and, between two and three o'clock on Saturday morning, (the 14th,) he awoke Mrs. Washington and told her that he was very unwell. He then had great difficulty in *breathing, speaking, and swallowing.*

These are the symptoms which are characteristics, the essential characteristics, of his disease. They continued till his death, which took place between 10 and 11 o'clock in the following night. There seem to have been some hours during which he did not swallow anything, in consequence of the distress attending any effort to do it. It was also so difficult to speak, that he did that only when he thought it important, and as briefly as was consistent with his habitual care to be distinct and definite in his expressions. It was the breathing, however, which caused him most distress. In regard to that the patient cannot choose, as he can in respect to speaking and swallowing. The efforts which he was compelled to make in breathing were extremely distressing, and occasioned great restlessness;—the more because his strongest efforts were insufficient to supply his lungs with as much air as his system had need of. It was from the inability to do this that death ensued. He was in fact strangulated by the closure of the windpipe, as much as if a tight cord had been twisted around his neck. His intellect remained unclouded, and it is needless to say that he showed to the last those strong and great characteristics of mind and heart, by which his whole life had been marked.

What was this disease which cut down a strong man in so short a time? It was such as has cut down very many, no doubt, in times past; but it is a rare disease. It had not, at the time of Washington's death, been clearly described, so as to be distinguished from other diseases about the throat. It is now well known under the name of *acute laryngitis;*—inflammation of the larynx,—the upper part of the windpipe. ·It was about 1810 that this morbid affection was first brought into notice and distinctly described by Dr. Matthew Baillie, of London, confessedly, while he lived, at the head of his profession in that great city. He published two cases seen by himself, both of them within a short period, both in

medical men, and one of them a very dear friend of his.
To these he added a third case reported to him by a practitioner in London, which was evidently like the other two.
He ascertained the morbid changes, by which these persons
had been suddenly deprived of life, by examinations after
death. It was ascertained by these examinations, as it has
been by many made since in similar cases, that the disease
consists in an inflammation in the mucous membrane of the
whole larynx, including the epiglottis; but that this inflammation is not limited to the mucous membrane. It extends
to the cellular membrane subjacent to the other, indeed to all
the soft parts, including the muscles; and perhaps, in some
degree, to the cartilages. From these morbid changes the
epiglottis is disabled from the free and ready motion essential
to its office, which is that of guarding the windpipe from
the admission of substances passing through the pharynx.
Hence one of the difficulties in swallowing, probably the
greatest. In such a state the attempt to swallow any substance, liquid or solid, would be attended by an instinctive
effort of the epiglottis to shut up the larynx, as it always
does in health during the act of swallowing. But this instinctive effort must cost great pain; and it is an effort
which could not succeed in the most severe state of the disease. Thus the principal difficulty in swallowing is explained. Another difficulty in swallowing arises from the
state of the pharynx. The inflammation of the larynx passing over its posterior part, in some if not all cases, spreads
to the pharynx, and disables that part from performing its
office in carrying down the liquids or solids brought to it.

Just below the entrance to the larynx we find the delicate
structures belonging to the organ of the voice, and here is
the narrowest part of the·air tube. In these parts, a common acute inflammation of their mucous membrane will cause
soreness and hoarseness; but when the disease extends to

the subjacent cellular membrane, so that all these parts are thickened by the distention of the small bloodvessels, and the more if there take place an effusion of any fluid into this cellular membrane, it is seen at once how these soft parts must be swollen. Now this swelling occasions a difficulty, if not an impossibility, of motion in the delicate parts belonging to the organ of the voice, and accounts for the difficulty and at length the impossibility of speaking. At the same time we see how the passage of the air is impeded, and at last entirely obstructed, producing the difficulty of breathing and at length the strangulation.

Thus this disease, so suddenly destructive of life, is among the most simple in its nature. One readily understands that his fingers may be inflamed, that is, become red, swollen, indurated in all the soft parts, and painful, to such a degree as to make motion in them very difficult and at length impossible. But all this may take place without interfering with functions important to life. But let the organs, by which the voice is formed and through which the air must be passed for the supply of the lungs,— the organs through which the breath of life must have an open road,— let these organs be swollen and rigid so as to block up this passage, and we readily comprehend that life may be arrested in young or old, in the strong as well as in the feeble, in a very short space of time. It follows that the only question in a disease of this kind, as it occurs in adults, is whether we can prevent or remove the fatal obstruction which has been described as characteristic of this disease.

There are, however, some further remarks to be made on the disease, before discussing the treatment of it. Any one conversant with the subject will see at once how much acute laryngitis resembles the common affection which we all know as a sore throat from a cold. Though the words *a cold* are employed with reference to any disease which is

thought to arise from an exposure to a change of tempera-
ture, or to cold and damp weather, they are most commonly
used in reference to an attack in the nose, or in the windpipe. These are called colds in the head, or colds in the
throat. The cold in the throat is marked by a sense of
slight soreness in that part, (especially felt in deglutition and
in coughing), and by hoarseness in the voice. Some cough
soon follows and presently an expectoration of matter, at
first watery and afterwards thick and glutinous, and more or
less opaque. In these cases there is an inflammation of the
mucous membrane of the larynx. The disease may begin
in the nasal passages, when it is commonly called a cold in
the head, or a nasal catarrh; and this does most frequently
take place first; but whichever part is affected first, the inflammation may extend from this to the other. Further,
when the larynx is affected, the inflammation may also pass
downward to the bronchi, which are the ramifications of the
windpipe in the lungs. Then the disease gets the name of
pulmonary catarrh, or bronchitis.

To one who understands the above statement, it will be
plain that the cold in the throat, when there take place
soreness in the throat, hoarseness, a slight difficulty in deglutition, and more or less cough,—in other words, *a hoarse sore
throat*, is the same thing as the acute laryngitis. It is assur-
edly the same thing, except in degree. In the disease first
described, the *laryngitis*, the inflammation is more severe,
and it is not confined to the mucous membrane, but extends
to the other tissues. The mucous membrane may be called
an internal skin; and like the skin it is connected with
other parts by a cellular membrane. Now if the skin be
inflamed in its external surface only, in one man, and in
another an inflammation of the skin should pass through it
into the subjacent cellular membrane, the swelling would be
much more in this last case than in the first. The greater

swelling in the second case would be attended with more general affection of the system than would occur in the first one. So far the difference between the common affection of the larynx, in ordinary colds, and that in the severe disease under consideration, is illustrated by the supposed inflammation in the skin in the two men. But there is one great difference. The swelling of the skin is not productive of any serious inconvenience; not so in the larynx. That is the tube through which the air passes to the lungs in respiration, and in one part the passage is very narrow. In this part the swelling must occupy the calibre of the tube; in fatal cases it fills up the air passage; and the effect of this is the same as if a cord were tied very tightly around the neck. As the passage is filling up, the air passes with more and more difficulty, and at last it cannot pass at all. Even this, however, does not state quite the whole. In the last hours of life, the lungs do not get air enough to produce the requisite change in the blood; and likewise the carbonic acid gas, which is an excretion from the blood, and is usually discharged at once from the lungs, is retained in some measure and acts as a poison. From this imperfect renewal of the blood, if we may use the expression, arises the livid countenance in the last hours; and under this state of the blood every part of the body is constantly losing its vigor. Thus, before the larynx is absolutely blocked up, the muscles of respiration become incapable of the effort requisite to expand the thorax, and death ensues, although there may be a very small passage still left open at the last moment of life.

We are prepared now to consider the treatment proper in acute laryngitis, in connection with that adopted in the case under consideration. It has been thought by many persons, medical and non-medical, that General Washington was not treated judiciously; and some, perhaps, believe that by a different treatment his life might have been preserved. Sixty years have passed since his decease, and the disease, which was fatal to him, is understood now much more perfectly than it was in 1799. To what result have we arrived? Has any treatment proved to be more successful than that adopted in his case? He was bled, he was blistered, and calomel and antimony were administered internally. Whether these remedies were employed early enough, and whether to too great an extent, or not sufficiently, are questions to which we will return presently.

What was the treatment adopted by Dr. Baillie in the cases of his medical friends? He directed bleeding, both general and local, and his patients not only agreed with him, but, being medical men, directed it for themselves in his absence. This happened at a period comparatively near to that of Washington's case.

What do the best teachers say at the present day? To answer this question fully and accurately would require great research. One need not, however, hesitate to say, generally, that they recommend bleeding and blistering. In addition, the English teachers advise the use of mercurials carried to the point of salivation, and our own did the same until very lately. Some of them, perhaps, do it now. Some, if not many, would add antimony and opium to the calomel, or other preparations of mercury.

We believe that the lectures by Dr. Watson of London are received, as good authority, by as many persons who speak the English language, as the work of any writer of our time on the theory and practice of medicine. In the last edition of his lectures he advises bleeding freely at an early period of acute laryngitis, with the qualifications which every discreet and experienced practitioner would assent to. So far, then, it would seem that the treatment adopted by Dr. Craik and his medical coadjutors is the same, which has been, and is now directed by physicians of the first standing.

Let us look into this matter somewhat, and see whether bloodletting in acute laryngitis appears to be a rational practice. To what cause is the danger to life to be attributed in this disease? The answer has already been given. The danger arises from the filling up of a part of the windpipe. In what way, or by what material is the windpipe filled up? By an extra quantity of blood in the small vessels of the part, similar to what most persons may have seen in a violent inflammation of the external surface of the eye. By this blood in the first instance, and in part, is the tube filled up; but further, by the effusion under the mucous membrane of the larynx of a watery liquid, called serum, or serous fluid. When a man is bled largely he usually becomes pale. This happens because the small vessels of the external surface contract under the loss of blood, and the skin is seen to be white, or sallow, according to the complexion of the individual. If, in the disease under consideration, the small bloodvessels in the morbid part will contract as those of the skin do, after the abstraction of blood, we may hope for relief, as long as that contraction is maintained. Not only so; it will be found that if this contraction takes place in the diseased part, the effusion of serous fluid is more readily absorbed than it would otherwise be.

It must be confessed that the effect, here described, on the small bloodvessels in the morbid part, is not certain to take place in consequence of the loss of blood. The success of the measure depends mainly on the period of the disease, at which the bleeding takes place. The chance of success is great in the very beginning of the inflammatory process; but it is less, the later the period at which the remedy is employed. There is not, however, any other measure by which effectual relief is so likely to be produced as by blood-

letting. If anything else can be equally effectual, in so short
a space of time, it must be some local applications to the part
affected.   There are cases of disease in the larynx, where
nitrate of silver and other articles may perhaps be applied to
the parts affected, with great benefit. But in the irritable
state of the part in question, in this acute disease, such applications must be attended with very great difficulty, and
apparently with great hazard. The success of this treatment
in cases of ulceration in the mucous membrane of the larynx,
in a chronic disease, does not prove what would happen in
the acute disease under consideration.

But there is a difficulty which ordinarily attends the bleeding in this disease, to which may be attributed the failure in
the largest proportion of cases, in which it has been tried.
It is that the disease usually commences under the familiar
form of a common cold in the throat, so that at first no alarm
is felt. Nor ought there to be an alarm in such a case. It
has been shown above that such an inflammation as occurs
in a common *hoarse cold* may suddenly increase in importance by extending from the mucous membrane or tissue, to
the surrounding tissues, especially to the subjacent cellular
membrane. Then comes the tumefaction, which, acting me-
chanically, blocks up the passage of the air into the lungs. It
is in this first stage, before the fatal extension of the inflammation has occurred, that the disease might be the most
easily arrested. But who would advise the active treatment
requisite for this purpose in every case of a *hoarse cold*,
which is the first stage? In every such case the severe disease may ensue. But what is the chance that it will ensue?
A very large proportion of persons, probably three quarters
of the community among us, have such a cold once a year,
and not a few have such an attack twice or three times in a
year; but the change into the severe disease, called acute
laryngitis, is among the most rare occurrences. It does not

take place in one case out of a million. But if it happened in one case in a hundred, it would not be justifiable to resort to a severe treatment in each one of a hundred cases, in order to save one of them from the fatal change. There is no doubt that every discreet man would choose to incur the slight hazard of the severe disease, rather than to resort to a copious bleeding every time he had a hoarse sore throat. Washington was evidently familiar with a cold in his throat in his sixty-eighth year, as other men are. He probably had never suspected the possible issue of such a cold. But if he had been told that the chance of such an issue was one in a million, or even one in a hundred, would he have consented to a copious bleeding? We think not.

Here we see the real difficulty. At the time when the danger is manifested, the disease is not strictly new; it has not just commenced. In looking over the histories of cases of acute laryngitis we find that the disease, under the form of a hoarse cold, has existed from a few hours to a few days, before it arrives at the state when danger to life is suspected. It cannot be said that the bleeding, at that stage of the disease, can be relied on, as it might have been in the very commencement. Yet this remedy, even then, affords a chance of relief, and the more when the disease has not remained long in the first stage. In Washington's case the first stage was of short duration. Bleeding was resorted to early, by his own direction. But that bleeding was nominal. His wife objected to it, because the patient was old, and the bleeding had not been directed by a physician. We must give her the credit of exercising a wise caution. Of course she did not understand the nature of the disease; she did not suspect how rapidly it was pressing forward to a fatal termination. Even the delay of the three or four hours which had already passed away since he waked her up in the night, was a most serious loss. When Dr. Craik reached him some hours afterwards, he prescribed a new venesection. He was right; it is in such circumstances that the *anceps remedium* is justifiable.   What would medical critics, what would posterity have said, if this good doctor, when such a patient was in his hands, in imminent danger from an affection which was manifestly due to inflammation, had folded his arms, and said, " There is no possibility of giving relief; but you may let him inhale the vapor from some herb tea "?

Although bloodletting is the great remedy, there are other modes of treatment which may be employed in aid of it, or without it. Calomel and antimony, usually with the addition of opium, are thought by many physicians to be proper articles for the relief of this laryngitis. Colonel Lear says that calomel and antimony were given to General Washington, but he does not say in what doses, nor whether more than once. There is not any reason to believe that they were given in large doses; though I think Dr. Craik and his coadjutors have been reproached on this score. In 1799 the use of mercurials in inflammatory diseases was very rare, I believe, in Great Britain, though it was very common in this country. At the present day the reverse is true. At least in New England the practice is now relied on much less than in old England. Fashions change, it must be acknowledged, in medicine as in other things. Probably the result, at the end of another fifty years, will be that mercurials will not be administered in either country as freely as they have been heretofore, but that they will not be abandoned altogether.

It would not be well to go further into the subject on this occasion. We have considered the bloodletting more fully perhaps than was quite necessary, but it has been to defend the reputation of Dr. Craik and his medical friends, who we think did as well, at least, as any of their critics would have done in the like case. We must acknowledge an unwillingness not to think well of Dr. Craik, who was the personal friend of Washington through his life.

Passing by some other modes of treatment of acute laryngitis, we should not omit to notice one, on which much reliance is placed at the present day, when it becomes obvious that all other remedies are ineffectual. This consists in an opening into the trachea, below the diseased part. In this way life may be prolonged while a chance is afforded for the subsidence of the disease by a natural process, after which the wound may be allowed to heal up. This practice has been resorted to with success in various instances of obstructions in the windpipe, and especially of late in croup. In this disease of children and in the acute laryngitis of adults, it is important that the surgical operation should be performed before the vital powers have been too much exhausted by the painful and wearing struggles for life.

But it is time to bring this note to a close. On some points the writer has gone into a minute statement of particulars, and into a discussion of principles, as to the pathology and as to the therapeutics. But this has been done only so far as seemed to him necessary to make the subject understood by non-professional men; not with any pretence to bring into view all that relates to the disease or its treatment. If he seem to have lingered on the subject too long, it will be remembered that the interest which is inspired by every circumstance in the life of Washington, attaches, with melancholy intensity, to the disease by which it was suddenly brought to a close.

Boston, March, 1860.

No. II.

[The following is the official inventory of the personal property at Mount Vernon, taken by the sworn appraisers after the decease of General Washington. It includes, as will be perceived, a list of the books in his library. Some portions of the inventory, containing the appraisal of the articles in most of the bedrooms and in the various domestic offices, and of the implements of husbandry and stock on the farms, are omitted for want of room. The columns are not footed up in consequence of these omissions, but the sum total on the last page includes the entire amount of the inventory.]

AN INVENTORY OF ARTICLES AT MOUNT VERNON, WITH THEIR APPRAISED VALUE ANNEXED.

In the New Room.

	$	cts.
2 Large Looking-glasses	200	00
4 Silver-plated Lamps, &c.	60	00
6 Mahogany Knife Cases	100	00
2 Sideboards, on each of which is an Image and China Flower-pot	160	00
27 Mahogany Chairs at $10	270	00
2 Candle Stands	40	00
2 Fire-screens	40	00
2 Elegant Lustres	120	00
2 Large gilt-framed Pictures, representing the Fall of Rivers	160	00
4 do. representing Watercourses, &c.	240	00
1 do. small Likeness of General Washington	100	00
1 do. Louis XVI.	50	00
2 do. Prints, Death of Montgomery	100	00
2 do. Battle of Bunker's Hill	100	00

	$	cts.
2 Large gilt-framed Pictures, Dead Soldier	45	00
1 Likeness of St. John	15	00
1 do. Virgin Mary	15	00
4 Small Prints (one under each Lamp)	8	00
1 Painting, Moonlight	60	00
5 China Jars	100	00
All the Images	100	00
1 Mat	10	00
Window Curtains	100	00
2 Round Stools	6	00
Shovel, Tongs, Poker, and Fender	20	00

In the *Little Parlor*.

	$	cts.
1 Looking-glass	30	00
1 Tea-table	8	00
1 Settee	15	00
10 Windsor Chairs	20	00
2 Prints representing Storms at Sea	30	00
1 do. A Sea-fight between Paul Jones of the *Bon Homme Richard* and Captain Pearson of the *Serapis*	10	00
1 do. The distressed Situation of Quebec, &c.	15	00
2 do. : one The Whale Fishery of Davis's Straits and the other of the Greenlands	20	00
1 Likeness of General Washington in an oval Frame	4	00
1 do. Doctor Franklin	4	00
1 do. Lafayette	4	00
1 Gilt Frame of wrought Work containing Chickens in a Basket	20	00
1 do. Likeness of a Deer	5	00
1 Painted Likeness of an Aloe	2	00
6 Others of different Paintings	12	00

		$	cts.
1 Carpet		10	00
2 Window Curtains		5	00
Andirons, Tongs, and Fender		6	00

In the Front Parlor.

	$	cts.
1 Elegant Looking-glass	60	00
1 Tea-table	15	00
1 Sofa	70	00
11 Mahogany Chairs	99	00
3 Lamps, two with Mirrors	40	00
5 China Flower-pots	50	00
1 Gilt Frame, Marquis Lafayette and Family	100	00
1 do. General Washington	50	00
1 do. Mrs. Washington	50	00
1 do. Mr. Lear	80	00
1 do. Mrs. Law	70	00
1 do. Mrs. Washington's two Children	50	00
1 do. Mrs. Washington's Daughter when grown	10	00
1 Small oval Frame (gilt) containing the Likeness of Washington Custis	10	00
1 do. George W. Lafayette	10	00
1 do. General Washington	10	00
1 do. Mrs. Washington	10	00
1 Gilt square Frame, the Likeness of Miss Custis	10	00
1 do. emblematic of General Washington	10	00
2 Window Curtains	16	00
1 Carpet	80	00
Andirons, Shovel, Tongs, &c.	8	00

In the Dining-Room.

	$	cts.
1 Oval Looking-glass	15	00
1 Mahogany Sideboard	23	00
1 Tea-table	2	00

	$	cts.
2 Dining-tables	30	00
1 Large Case	10	00
2 Knife Cases	6	00
10 Mahogany Chairs	50	00
1 Large gilt Frame, Print, The Death of the late Earl of Chatham	50	00
1 do. General Wolfe	15	00
1 do. Penn's Treaty with Indians	15	00
1 do. Rittenhouse	5	00
1 do. Doctor Franklin	10	00
1 do General Washington	7	00
1 do. General Greene	7	00
1 do. America	6	00
1 do. General Lafayette, or Conclusion of the late War	7	00
1 do. General Wayne	7	00
1 do. Washington Family of Mount Vernon	20	00
1 do. Alfred visiting his Noblemen	9	00
1 do. Alfred dividing his Loaf with the Pilgrim	9	00
1 Carpet	2	00
Window Curtains	2	00
Water Pitcher		50
Andirons, Shovel, Tongs, and Fender	8	00

In the Bedroom.

	$	cts.
1 Looking-glass	10	00
1 Small Table	5	00
1 Bed, Bedstead, and Mattress	50	00
4 Mahogany or Walnut Chairs	8	00
1 Large gilt Frame containing A Battle fought by Cavalry	30	00
Window Curtains and Blinds	1	50
1 Carpet	5	00

	$	cts.
Andirons, Shovel, Tongs, and Fender · · · · · · · · · ·	4	00

In the Passage.

	$	cts.
14 Mahogany Chairs ·	70	00
1 Print, Diana dec'd by Venus· · · · · · · · · · · · · · · · ·	5	00
1 do. Adonis carried off by Venus· · · · · · · · · · · · · ·	5	00
1 do. The dancing Shepherds · · · · · · · · · · · · · · · · ·	5	00
1 do. Morning ·	5	00
1 do. Evening ·	8	00
1 do. View of the River Po in Italy· · · · · · · · · · · · ·	8	00
1 do. Constantine's Arch ·	8	00
1 do. General Washington ·	25	00
1 do. Key of Bastile with its Representation · · · · · · ·	10	00
1 Thermometer· ·	5	00
4 Images over the Door· ·	20	00
1 Spy-glass ·	5	00

In the Closet under the Staircase.

	$	cts.
1 Fire-screen· ·	2	00
1 Machine to scrape Shoes on · · · · · · · · · · · · · · · · ·	2	00

In the Piazza.

	$	cts.
30 Windsor Chairs ·	30	00

From the Foot of the Staircase to the Second Stairs.

	$	cts.
1 Gilt Frame, Print, Musical Shepherds · · · · · · · · · ·	10	00
1 do. Moonlight· ·	10	00
1 do. Thunder-storm ·	10	00
1 do. Battle of Bunker Hill ·	5	00
1 do. Death of Montgomery ·	15	00

In the Passage on the Second Floor.

	$	cts.
1 Looking-glass· ·	4	00

In the First Room on the Second Floor.

	$	cts.
1 Dressing-table	8	00
6 Mahogany Chairs	15	00
Bed, Bedstead, and Curtains	75	00
Window Curtains	1	00
1 Large Looking-glass	15	00
1 Print, Gainsborough Forest	8	00
1 do. Nymphs Bathing	8	00
1 do. Village	6	00
1 do. Storm	7	00
1 Carpet	5	00
Wash-basin and Pitcher	1	00
Andirons, Shovel, Tongs, and Fender	5	00

In the Second Room.

1 Arm-chair	6	00
Bedstead, Bed, Curtains, and Window Curtains	70	00
1 Looking-glass	15	00
1 Dressing-table	8	00
Likeness of General Lafayette	50	00
1 Carpet	10	00
4 Chairs	6	00
Wash-basin and Pitcher	1	00
Andirons, Shovel, Tongs, and Fender	4	00

In the Third Room.

6 Mahogany Chairs	24	00
1 Bed, Bedstead, and Curtains	85	00
Window Curtains	1	00
Chest of Drawers	15	00
1 Looking-glass	6	00
1 Wash-stand, Basin, and Pitcher	4	00
Carpet	7	00

	$	cts
1 Print, The Young Herdsman	5	50
1 do. The Flight	5	50
1 do. Morning	5	50
1 do. Evening	5	50
Andirons, Shovel, Tongs, and Fender	4	50

In the Fourth Room.

	$	cts
5 Mahogany Chairs	16	00
1 Bed, Bedstead, and Curtains	77	50
Window Curtains	2	00
1 Close Chair	6	00
1 Pine Dressing-table	1	00
Carpet	10	00
1 Large Looking-glass	15	00
1 Print, Sun Rising	6	00
1 do. Sun Setting	6	00
1 do. Cupid's Pastime	6	00
1 do. Cottage	6	00
1 do. Herdsman	6	00
Wash-basin and Pitcher	1	50
Andirons, Shovel, Tongs, and Fender	4	50

In the Small Room.

	$	cts
1 Dressing-table	3	00
1 Wash-stand	4	00
3 Windsor Chairs	1	50
1 Bed and Bedstead	40	00
1 Dressing-glass	3	00

Glass and China in the China Closet and that Up-stairs, and also that in the Cellar· · · · · · · · 850 00

*   *   *   *   *   *

In the Room Mrs. Washington now keeps.

		$	cts.
1	Bedstead and Mattress	50	00
1	Oval Looking-glass	10	00
1	Fender	2	00
	Andirons, Shovel, and Tongs	2	00
3	Chairs	3	00
1	Table	3	00
1	Carpet	3	00

In Mrs. Washington's old Room.

1	Bed, Bedstead, and Curtains	70	00
1	Glass	2	00
1	Dressing-table	6	00
1	Writing-table	25	00
1	Writing Chair	2	00
1	Easy Chair	10	00
2	Mahogany Chairs	4	00
	A Timepiece	100	00
1	Chest of Drawers	30	00
6	Paintings of Mrs. Washington's Family	60	00
5	Small Drawings	2	50
1	Picture, Countess of Huntingdon		75
1	do. General Knox	1	00
1	do. A Parson	1	00
5	Small Pictures	2	00

* * * * * *

In the Study.

7	Swords and Blades	120	00
4	Canes	40	00
7	Guns	35	00
11	Spy-glasses	110	00

	$	cts.
1 Tin Canister of Drawing-paper		50
Trumbull's Prints	36	00
1 Case of Surveying Instruments	10	00
1 Travelling Ink Case	3	00
1 Globe	5	00
1 Chest of Tools	15	00
1 Box containing two Paper Moulds	25	00
1 Picture	3	00
1 Bureau	7	00
1 Dressing-table	40	00
1 Tambour Secretary	80	00
1 Walnut Table	5	00
1 Copying-press	30	00
1 Compass, Staff, and two Chains	30	00
1 Case of Dentist's Instruments	10	00
1 Old Copying-press	11	00
2 Sets Money Weights	20	00
1 Telescope	50	00
1 Box of Paints, &c.	16	00
1 Bust of General Washington in Plaster, from the Life	100	00
1 do. Marble	50	00
1 Profile in Plaster	25	00
2 Seals with Ivory Handles	8	00
1 Pocket Compass		50
1 Brass Level	10	00
1 Japan Box containing a Mason's Apron	40	00
1 Small Case containing three Straw Rings; one Farmer's Luncheon-box	1	71
1 Silk Sash (Military)	20	00
1 Velvet Housing for a Saddle and Holsters, trimmed with Silver Lace	5	00
1 Piece of Oil-cloth containing Orders of Masonry	50	00

	$	cts.
Some Indian Presents	5	00
1 Bust in Plaster of Paul Jones	20	00
2 Pine Writing-tables	4	00
1 Circular Chair	20	00
1 Box of Military Figures	2	00
1 Brass Model Cannon	15	00
2 Brass Candlesticks	2	00
2 Horsewhips	4	00
1 Pair of Steel Pistols	50	00
1 Copper Wash-basin		75
1 Chest and its Contents, &c.	100	00
1 Arm Chair	2	00
1 Writing-desk and Apparatus	5	00
1 (Green) Field-book		25
Balloon Flag	1	00
Tongs, Shovel, and Fender	1	00
A Painted Likeness, Lawrence Washington	10	00
1 Oval Looking-glass	2	00
3 Pair of Pistols	50	00

In the Iron Chest.

	$	cts.
Stock of the U. S. { 6 per cent. 8746 8746 } Dr. deferred 1878 } 2500 } 3 per cent. 2946 }	6,246	00
25 Shares Stock of the Bank of Alexandria	5,000	00
24 do. do. Potomac Company (@ £100 stg.)	10,666	00
Cash	254	70
1 Set of Shoe and Knee Buckles, Paste in Gold	250	00
1 Pair of Shoe and Knee Buckles, Silver	5	00
2 Gold Cincinnati Eagles	30	00
1 Diamond do.	387	00
1 Gold Watch, Chain, two Seals, and a Key	175	00
1 Compass in Brass Case		50

	$	cts
1 Gold Box presented by the Corporation of New York	100	00
5 Shares of James River Stock @ $100	500	00
170 Shares of Columbia Bank Stock @ $40	6,800	00
1 Large Gold Medal of General Washington	150	00
1 Gold Medal of St. Patrick Society	8	00
1 Ancient Medal (another Metal)	2	00
11 Medals in a Case	50	00
1 Large Medal of Paul Jones	4	00
3 Other Metal Medals	1	00
1 Brass Engraving of the Arms of the U. States	10	00
1 Pocket Compass	5	00
1 Case of Instruments, Parallel Rule, &c.	17	50
1 Pocket-book	5	00

Library.

	$	cts
American Encyclopædia, 18 vols. 4to.	150	00
Skombrand's Dictionary, 1 do.	7	50
Memoir of a Map Hindostan, 1 do. 4to.	8	00
Young's Travels, 1 do.	4	00
Johnson's Dictionary, 2 do.	10	00
Guthrie's Geography, 2 do.	20	00
Elements of Rigging, (?) 2 do.	20	00
Principles of Taxation, 1 do.	2	00
Luzac's Oration, 1 do.	1	00
Mawe's Gardener, 1 do.	4	00
Jeffries's Aërial Voyage, 1 do.	1	00
Beacon Hill, 1 do.	1	00
Memoirs of the American Academy (one of which is a Pamphlet), 2 do.	3	00
Duhamel's Husbandry, 1 do.	2	00
Langley on Gardening, 1 do.	2	00
Price's Carpenter, 1 do.	1	00

	$	cts.
Count de Grasse, 1 vol.	1	00
Miller's Gardener's Dictionary, 1 do.	5	00
Gibson's Diseases of Horses, 1 do.	3	00
Rumford's Essays	3	00
Miller's Tracts, 1 vol. 8vo.	2	00
Rowley's Works, 4 do.	12	00
Robertson's Charles V., 4 do.	16	00
Gordon's History of America, 4 do.	12	00
Gibbon's Roman Empire, 6 do.	18	00
Stanyan's Grecian History, 2 do.	2	00
Adam's Rome, 2 do.	4	00
Anderson's Institute, 1 do.	2	00
Robertson's America, 2 do.	4	00
Ossian's Poems, 1 do.	2	00
Humphreys's Works, 1 do.	3	00
King of Prussia's Works, 13 do.	26	00
Gillies's Frederick, 1 do.	1	50
Goldsmith's Natural History, 8 do.	12	00
Locke on Understanding, 2 do.	3	00
Shipley's Works, 2 do.	4	00
Buffon's Natural History abridged, 2 do.	4	00
Ramsay's History, 2 do.	2	00
The Bee (thirteenth volume missing), 18 do.	34	00
Sully's Memoirs, 6 do.	9	00
Fletcher's Appeal, 1 do.	1	00
History of Spain, 2 do. 8vo.	3	00
Jortin's Sermons, 2 do.	2	00
Chapman on Education, 1 do.		75
Smith's Wealth of Nations, 3 do.	4	50
History of Louisiana, 2 do.	2	00
Warren's Poems, 1 do.		50
Junius's Letters, 1 do.	1	00
City Addresses, 1 do.	1	0C

	$	cts.
Conquest of Canaan, 1 vol.	1	00
Shakspeare's Works, 1 do.	2	00
Antidote to Deism, 2 do.	1	00
Memoirs of 2500, 1 do.		75
Forest's Voyage, 1 do. 4to.	3	00
Don Quixote, 4 do.	12	00
Ferguson's Roman History, 3 do.	12	00
Watson's History of Philip II., 1 do.	4	00
Barclay's Apology, 1 do.	3	00
Uniform of the Forces of Great Britain in 1742, 1 do.	20	00
Otway's Art of War, 1 do.	3	00
Political States of Europe, 8 do. 8vo.	20	00
Winchester's Lectures, 4 do.	6	00
Principles of Hydraulics, 2 do.	2	00
Leigh on Opium, 1 do. 8vo.		75
Heath's Memoirs, 1 do.	2	00
American Museum, 10 do.	15	00
Vertot's Rome, 2 do.	2	00
Harte's Gustavus, 2 do.	2	00
Moore's Navigation, 1 do.	2	00
Graham on Education, 1 do.	2	00
History of the Mission among the Indians in North America, 1 do.	2	00
French Constitution, 1 do.	1	50
Winthrop's Journal, 1 do.	1	50
American Magazine, 1 do. 8vo.	4	00
Watts's Views, 1 do. 4to.	20	00
History of Marshal Turenne, 2 do. 8vo.	2	00
Ramsay's Revolution of South Carolina, 2 do.	2	00
History of Quadrupeds, 1 do.	1	50
Carver's Travels, 1 do.	1	50
Moore's Italy, 2 do.	3	00
Moore's France, 2 do.	3	00

	$	cts
Chastellux's Travels, 1 vol.	1	00
Chastellux's Voyages, 1 do.	1	00
Volney's Travels, 2 do.	3	00
Volney's Ruins, 1 do.	1	50
Warville's Voyage, in French, 3 do.	3	00
Warville on the Relation of France to the U. States	1	00
Miscellanies, 1 vol. 4to.	1	00
Fulton on Small Canals and Iron Bridges, 1 do.	3	00
Liberty, a Poem, 1 do.		50
Hazard's Collection of State Papers, 2 do	5	00
Young's Travels, 2 do.	4	00
West's Discourse, 1 do.	2	00
A Statement of the Representation of England and Wales, 1 do.		50
Miscellanies, 2 do.	2	00
Political Pieces, 1 do.	1	00
Treaties, 1 do.		50
Annual Register for 1781, 1 do. 8vo.		75
Masonic Constitution, 1 do. 4to.	1	00
Smith's Constitutions, 1 do.		50
Preston's Poems, 2 do.	1	00
History of the United States, 1796, 1 do. 8vo.		50
Parliamentary Debates, 12 do.	6	00
Mair's Book-keeping, 1 do.	1	50
Miscellanies, 1 do.	1	00
Proceedings of the East India Company, 1 do. fol.	4	00
Ladies' Magazine, 2 do. 8vo.	3	00
Parliamentary Register, 7 do.	3	50
Pryor's Documents, 2 do.	2	00
Remembrancer, 6 do.	3	00
European Magazine, 2 do.	3	00
Columbian do., 5 do.	10	00
American do., 1 do.	2	00

	$	cts.
New York Magazine, 1 vol.	2	00
Christian's do., 1 do.	2	00
Walker on Magnetism, 1 do.		50
Monroe's View of the Executive, 1 do.		75
Massachusetts Magazine, 2 do.	4	00
A Five Minutes' Answer to Paine's Letter to General Washington, 1 do.	1	00
Political Tracts, 1 do.	2	00
Proceedings on Parliamentary Reform, 1 do.	2	00
Poems on Various Subjects, 1 do.		50
Plays, &c., 1 do.		75
Annual Register, 3 do.	4	50
Botanico-Medical Dissertation, 1 do.		25
Oracle of Liberty, 1 do.		25
Cadmus, 1 do.	1	00
Doctrine of Projectiles, 1 do.		50
Patricius the Utilist, 1 do. 8vo.		50
Abiman Rezon, 1 do.	1	50
Sharp on the Prophecies, 1 do.		75
Minto on Planets, 1 do.		50
Sharp on the English Tongue, 1 do.		50
Sharp on Limitation of Slavery, 1 do.	1	50
Sharp on the People's Rights, 1 do.	1	00
Sharp's Remarks, 1 do.		50
National Defence, 1 do.		50
Sharp's Free Militia, 1 do.		50
Sharp on Congressional Courts, 1 do.		75
Ahiman Rezon, 1 do.	1	00
Vision of Columbus, 1 do.		50
Wilson's Lectures, 1 do.		75
Miscellanies, 1 do.	1	00
The Contrast, A Comedy, 1 do.		75
Sharp, An Appendix on Slavery, 1 do.		50

	$	cts.
Muir's Trial, 1 vol.		75
End of Time, 1 do.		75
Erskine's View of the War, 1 do...........	1	00
Political Magazine, 3 do.	4	50
The Law of Nature, 1 do. 12mo.		75
Washington's Legacy, 1 do.................	1	00
Political Tracts, 1 do. 8vo.................	1	00
America, 1 do.	1	00
Proofs of a Conspiracy, 1 do...............	1	50
Mackintosh's Defence, 1 do:	1	00
Miscellanies, 1 do.	1	00
Mirabeau, 1 do.............................	1	00
Virginia Journal, 1 do. 4to.................	1	00
Miscellanies, 1 do. 8vo.	1	25
Poems, &c., 1 do. 4to......................	1	00
Morse's Geography, 1 do. 8vo.	2	00
Messages, &c., 1 do.	1	00
History of Ireland, 2 do.	2	00
Harte's Works, 1 do.	1	25
Political Pamphlets, 1 do.	1	00
Burns's Poems, 1 do.	2	00
Political Tracts, 1 do......................		75
Miscellanies, 1 do.	1	00
Higgins on Cements, 1 do.	1	00
Repository, 2 do.	3	00
Reign of George III., 1 do.................	1	00
Political Tracts, 1 do......................	1	25
Tar Water, 1 do.		75
Minot's History, 1 do......................		75
Mease on the Bite of a Mad Dog, 1 do......	1	75
Political Tracts, 1 do......................	1	00
Reports, 1 do..............................	1	50
Revolution of France, 1 do.	1	00

	$	cts
Essay on Property, 1 vol.	1	00
Sir Henry Clinton's Narrative, 1 do.	1	00
Lord North's Administration, 1 do.	1	50
Lloyd's Rhapsody, 1 do.	1	00
Tracts, 1 do.	1	00
Inland Navigation, 1 do.	1	00
Chesterfield's Letters, 1 do.	1	50
Smith's Constitutions, 1 do. 4to.	1	00
Morse's Geography, 2 do. 8vo.	4	00
Belknap's American Biography, 2 do.	3	00
Belknap's History of New Hampshire, 1 do.	2	00
Do. do. do., 3 do.	5	00
Minot's History of Massachusetts, 1 do.	2	00
Jenkinson's Collection of Treaties, 3 do.	6	00
District of Maine, 1 do. 8vo.	1	50
Gulliver's Travels, 2 do.	1	50
Tracts on Slavery, 1 do.	1	00
Priestley's Evidences, 1 do.	1	00
Life of Buncle, 2 do.	3	00
Webster's Essays, 1 do.	1	50
Bartram's Travels, 1 do.	2	00
Bossu's Travels, 2 do.	3	00
Situation of America, 1 do.	1	00
Jefferson's Notes, 1 do.	1	50
Coxe's View, 1 do.	1	50
Ossian's Poems, 1 do.	1	50
Adams on Globes, 1 do.	2	00
Pike's Arithmetic, 1 do.	2	00
Barnaby's Sermons and Travels, 1 do	1	00
Champion on Commerce, 1 do.	1	00
Brown's Bible, 1 do. fol.	15	00
Bishop Wilson's Bible, 3 do.	60	00
Bishop Wilson's Works, 1 do.	15	00

		$	cts.
Laws of New York, 2 vols.		12	00
Laws of Virginia, 2 do.		3	00
Middleton's Architecture, 1 do.		3	00
Miller's Naval Architecture, 1 do.		4	00
The Senator's Remembrancer, 1 do.		3	00
The Origin of the Tribes or Nations in America, 1 do. 8vo.			75
A Treatise on the Principles of Commerce between Nations, 1 do.			50
Annual Register, 1 do.			50
General Washington's Letters, 2 do.		4	00
Insurrection, 1 do.			50
American Remembrancer, 3 do.		1	50
Epistles for the Ladies, 1 do.			50
Discourses upon Common Prayer, 1 do.			25
The Trial of the Seven Bishops, 1 do. 8vo.			50
Lebroune's Surveyor, 1 do. fol.		1	00
Sharp's Sermons, 1 do. 8vo.			50
Muir's Discourses, 1 do.			75
Emblems Divine and Moral, 1 do.		1	00
Yorick's Sermons, 2 do.		1	00
D'Ivernois on Agriculture, Colonies, and Commerce, 1 do.			75
Pocket Dictionary, 1 do.			25
Prayer Book, 1 do.		1	50
Royal English Grammar, 1 do.			25
Principles of Trade compared, 1 do.			50
Dr. Morse's Sermon, 1 do.			50
Duché's Sermon, 1775, 1 do.			50
Sermons, 1 do.			50
Embassy to China, 1 do.		1	00
Warren's Poems, 1 do.		1	00
Sermons, 1 do.			25

	$ cts.
Humphrey Clinker, 1 vol.	25
Poems, 1 do.	50
Swift's Works, 1 do.	50
History of a Foundling, (3d vol. wanting,) 3 do.	1 50
Adventures of Telemachus, 2 do.	2 00
Nature Displayed, 1 do.	1 00
Solyman and Almenia, 1 do.	50
Plays, 1 do.	50
The High German Doctor, 1 do.	25
Benezet's Discourse, 1 do.	25
Life and Death of the Earl of Rochester, 1 do.	25
Journal of the Senate and House of Representatives, 9 do. fol.	27 00
Laws of the United States, 7 do.	28 00
Revised Laws of Virginia, 1 do.	10 00
Acts of Virginia Assembly, 5 do.	1 00
Cruttwell's Concordance, 1 do.	5 00
Dallas's Reports, 1 do. 8vo.	3 00
Swift's System, 2 do.	3 00
Journals of the Senate and House of Representatives, 3 do.	6 00
State Papers, 1 do.	2 00
Burn's Justice, 4 do.	12 00
Marten's Law of Nations, 1 do.	1 50
Views of the British Customs, 1 do.	1 00
Debates of Congress, 3 do.	4 50
Journals of Congress, 13 do.	40 00
Laws of the United States, 3 do.	6 00
Kirby's Reports, 1 do.	2 00
Virginia Justice, 1 do.	1 00
Virginia Laws, 1 do.	1 00
Dogge on Criminal Law, 3 do.	4 50
Laws of the United States, 2 do.	4 00

	$	cts.
Debates of the State of Massachusetts on the Constitution, 1 vol.		50
Sharp on the Law of Nature, 1 do.		25
Sharp on the Law of Retribution, 1 do.		25
Sharp on Libels and Juries, 1 do.		25
Acts of Congress, 1 do.		75
Debates of the Convention of Virginia, 1 do.		50
The Landlord's Law, 1 do. 12mo.		25
Attorney's Pocket-book, 2 do. 8vo.	1	00
President's Messages, 1 do.	2	00
Jay's Treaty, 1 do.		50
Debates of the Convention of Massachusetts, 1 do.		50
Law against Bankrupts, 1 do.		50
Debates in the Convention of Pennsylvania, 1 do.		50
Debates in the Convention of Virginia, 1 do.		50
Debates in the House of Representatives of the United States with respect to their power on Treaties, 1 do.		50
Sundry Pamphlets containing Messages from the President to Congress, &c.	1	00
Orations, 1 vol. 4to.		50
Gospel News, 1 do. 8vo.	1	00
Mosaical Creation, 1 do. 8vo.		75
Original and Present State of Man, 1 do.		50
Sermons, 2 do.	1	50
Political Sermons, 3 do.	2	25
Miscellanies, 1 do.		75
Ray on the Wisdom of God in Creation, 1 do.	1	00
Orations, 1 do.		75
Medical Tracts, 2 do.	1	50
Masonic Sermons, 1 do.		50
Miscellanies, 1 do.		75
Backus's History, 1 do.	1	00

	$	cts.
Sick Man Visited, 1 vol.		75
State of Man, 1 do.		75
Churchill's Sermon, 1 do.		75
Account of the Protestant Church, 1 do.		75
Exposition of the Thirty-Nine Articles, 1 do.	1	00
Dodington's Diary, 1 do.	1	00
Daveis' Cavalry, 1 do.	1	00
Simms's Military Course, 1 do.	1	00
Gentleman's Magazine, 3 do.	4	50
Library Catalogue, 1 do.	1	50
Transactions of the Royal Humane Society, 1 do.	3	00
Zimmermann's Survey, 1 do.		75
History of Barbary, 1 do.		75
Anson's Voyage round the World, 1 do.	1	00
Horseman and Farrier, 1 do.	1	00
Gordon's Geography, 1 do.	1	00
Kentucky, 1 do.		75
History of Virginia, 1 do.	1	00
American Revolution, 1 do.	1	00
Cincinnati, 1 do.	1	00
Political Tracts, 1 do.		75
Remarks on the Encroachments of the River Thames, 1 do.		50
Sharp on Crown Law, 1 do. 8vo.		50
Common Sense, &c., 1 do.		75
Hardy's Tables, 1 do.		75
Beauties of Sterne, 1 do.		75
Peregrine Pickle, 3 do.	1	50
M'Fingal, 1 do.		50
Memoirs of the noted Buckhorse, 2 do.	1	00
Odyssey, (Pope's translation of Homer,) 5 do.	3	00
Miscellanies, 3 do.	1	50
Fitzosborne's Letters, 1 do.		50

	$	cts.
Voltaire's Letters, 1 vol.		50
Guardian, 2 do.	1	00
Beauties of Swift, 1 do.		50
The Gleaner, 3 do.	3	00
Miscellanies, 2 do.	1	50
Lee's Memoirs, 1 do.	1	00
The Universalist, 1 do.	1	00
Chesterfield's Letters, 4 do.	2	00
Louis XV., 4 do.	3	00
Bentham's Panoption, 3 do.	2	00
Reason, &c., 1 do.		50
Tour through Great Britain, 4 do.	3	00
Female Fortune-Hunter, 3 do.	1	00
The Supposed Daughter, 3 do.	1	50
Gil Blas, 4 do.	3	00
Columbian Grammar, 1 do		50
Frazier's Assistant, 1 do.		50
Review of Cromwell's Life, 1 do.		75
Seneca's Morals, 1 do.		75
Travels of Cyrus, 1 do.		75
Miscellanies, 1 do.		75
Charles XII., 1 do.		50
Emma Corbet, (the 2d vol. wanting,) 2 do.	1	00
Pope's Works, 6 do. 12mo.	2	00
Foresters, 1 do.		50
Adams's Defence, 1 do. 8vo.		75
Butler's Hudibras, 1 do.	1	00
Spectator, 6 do.	3	00
New Crusoe, 1 do.		75
Philadelphia Gazette, 1 do. fol.	10	00
Pennsylvania Packet, 2 do.	12	00
Gazette of the United States, 10 do.	40	00
Atlas to Guthrie's Geography, 1 do.	40	00

	$	cts.
Moll's Atlas, 1 vol.	10	00
West India Atlas, 1 do.	20	00
General Geographer, 1 do.	30	00
Atlas of North America, 1 do.	10	00
Manœuvres, 1 do. 8vo.	1	00
Military Instructions, 1 do.		50
Count Saxe's Plan for New-modelling the French Army, 1 do.		50
Military Discipline, 1 do. 4to.	2	00
Prussian Evolutions, 1 do.	1	50
Code of Military Standing Resolutions, 2 do.	4	00
Field Engineer, 1 do. 8vo.	1	50
Army List, 1 do.		75
Prussian Evolutions, 1 do. 4to.	2	00
Leblond's Engineer, 2 do. 8vo.	3	00
Muller on Fortification, 1 do.	2	00
Essays on Field Artillery, by Anderson, 1 do.		75
A System of Camp Discipline, 1 do.	2	00
Essay on the Art of War, 1 do.	1	00
Treatise of Military Discipline, 1 do.	1	50
List of Military Officers, British and Irish in 1777, 1 do.		50
Vallancey on Fortification, 1 do.	1	50
Muller on Artillery, 1 do.	1	50
Muller on Fortification, 1 do.	2	00
Militia, 1 do. 8vo.	1	00
American Atlas, 1 do. fol.	4	00
Steuben's Regulations, 1 do. 8vo.		75
Traite de Cavalerie, 1 do. fol.	6	00
Truxtun on Latitude and Longitude, 1 do.	1	50
Ordinances of the King, 1 do.	2	00
Magnetic Atlas, 1 do.	1	00
Roads through England, 1 do. 8vo.	1	00
Carey's War Atlas, 1 vol. fol.		75

	$	cts
Caller's Survey of Roads, 1 do. 8vo.		50
Military Institutions for Officers, 1 do.		50
Norfolk Exercise, 1 do.		25
Advice of Officers of the British Army, 1 do.		25
Webb's Treatise on the Appointments of the Army, 1 do.		25
Acts of the Parliament respecting Militia, 1 do.		25
The Partisan, 1 do.		50
Anderson on Artillery, (in French,) 1 do.		25
List of Officers under Sir William Howe in America, 1 do.		25
The Military Guide, 1 do.		50
The Duties of Soldiers in General, 3 do.	1	50
Young's Tour, 2 do.	3	00
Young on Agriculture, (17 vols. full bound, 8 half bound, and 1 pamphlet,) 26 do.	50	00
Anderson on Agriculture, (1 vol. full bound, the others in boards,) 4 do.	8	00
Lisle's Observations on Husbandry, 2 do.	3	00
Museum Rusticum, 6 do.	10	00
Marshall's Rural Ornament, 2 do.	4	00
Barlow's Husbandry, 2 do.	3	00
Kennedy on Gardening, 2 do.	2	00
Hale on Husbandry, 4 do.	6	00
Sentimental Magazine, 5 do.	10	00
Price on the Picturesque, 2 do.	4	00
Agriculture, 2 do.	2	00
Miller's Gardener's Calendar, 1 do.	2	00
Rural Economy, 1 do. 8vo.	1	00
Agricultural Inquiries, 1 do.	1	00
Maxwell's Practical Husbandry, 1 do.	2	00
Boswell on Meadows, 1 do.	1	00

	$ cts.
Gentleman Farmer, 1 vol.	1 50
Practical Farmer, 1 do.	1 50
Millwright and Miller's Guide, 1 do.	2 00
Bordley on Husbandry, 1 do.	2 25
Sketches and Inquiries, 1 do.	2 00
Farmer's Complete Guide, 1 do.	1 00
The Solitary, or Carthusian Gardener, 1 do.	1 00
Homer's Iliad by Pope, (first two vols. wanting,) 4 do.	2 00
Don Quixote, 4 do.	3 00
Federalist, 2 do.	3 00
The World Displayed, (13th vol. wanting,) 19 do. 12mo.	9 50
Search's Essays, 2 do. 8vo.	2 00
Freneau's Poems, 1 do.	1 00
Cattle Doctor, 1 do.	75
Stephens's Directory, 1 do.	50
New System of Agriculture, 1 do.	50
Columbus's Discovery, 1 do.	25
Moore's Travels, 5 do.	4 00
Agricultural Society of New York, 1 do. 4to.	2 00
Transactions of the Agricultural Society of New York, 1 do.	1 00
Annals of Agriculture, 1 do.	2 00
Dundonald's Connection between Agriculture and Chemistry, 1 do.	1 00
Labors in Husbandry, 1 do.	1 00
Account of different Kind of Sheep, 1 do. 8vo.	50
The Hothouse Gardener, 1 do.	1 50
Historical Memoirs of Frederick II., 3 do.	1 00
Treatise of Peat Moss, 1 do.	50
Treatise on Bogs and Swampy Grounds, 1 do.	75
Complete Farmer, 1 do. fol.	6 00

$ cts.

Pamphlets,—

    Reports of the National Agricultural Society
       of Great Britain, 100 Nos. 4to.   25 00
    Massachusetts Magazine, 41 do. 8vo.   6 00
    New York Magazine, 38 do.   6 00
    London Magazine, 18 do.   3 00
    Political Magazine, 8 do.   1 00
    Universal Asylum, 9 do.   1 50
    Universal Magazine, 11 do.   1 50
    Country Magazine, 15 do.   2 00
    Monthly and Critical Reviews, 11 do.   2 00
    Gentleman's Magazine, 8 do.   1 00
    Congressional Register, 9 do.   1 00
    Miscellaneous Magazine, 27 do.   3 00
    Tom Paine's Rights of Man, 43 do.   15 00
    Miscellaneous Magazine, 27 do.   4 00

Books,—

    Hazard's Collection of State Papers, 2 vols.
       4to.   5 00
    Morse's American Gazetteer, 1 do. 8vo.   2 00
    Annals of Agriculture, (20 and 21,) 2 do.   3 00
    On the American Revolution, 1 do.   1 50
    15 Pamphlets, Annals of Agriculture,   2 50
    Judge Peters on Plaster of Paris, 1 vol.   1 50
    Belknap's Biography, 1 do.   1 50
    American Remembrancer, 1 do.   50
    Federalist, 2 do.   1 50
A Pamphlet, The Debate of Parliament on the Ar-
    ticles of Peace, 1 do.   25
History of the American War, in 17 pamphlets   1 50
Miscellaneous Pamphlets, 26 Nos.   2 00
Washington, a Poem   2 00
Alfieri, Bruto Primo, Italian Tragedy   1 00

$ cts.

Fragment of Politics and Literature, by Mandril-
   lon, (in French,) 1 vol. 8vo. 75
Revolution of France and Geneva, (in French,) 2 do.   2 00
History of the Administration of the Finances of
   the French Republic, 1 do. 50
History of the French Administration, 1 do. 75
The Social Compact, (in French,) 1 do. 25
Chastellux's Travels in North America, (in French,)
   2 do. 8vo. 1 50
1 Pamphlet, Of the French Revolution at Geneva . . 25
America Delivered, a Poem, (in French,) 2 vols. . . . 1 50
Sinclair's Statistics, (in French,) 1 do. 1 00
The Works of Monsieur Chamousset, (in French,)
   2 do. 4 00
Letters of American Farmer, (in French,) 3 do. 4 50
Germanicus, (in French,) 1 do. 25
Triumph of the New World, (in French,) 2 do. 1 50
United States of America, (in German,) 1 do. 1 50
Chastellux, Discourse on the Advantage of the Dis-
   covery of America, 1 do. 1 00
A German Book, 1 do. 25
The French Mercury, (in French,) 4 do. 3 00
Essay on Weights, Measures, &c., 2 do. 75
History of England, 2 do. 25
Political Journal, (in German,) 1 do. 50
Letters in French and English, 1 do. 25
History of the Holy Scriptures, 1 do. 25
History of Gil Blas, 2 do. 1 00
Telemachus, 2 do. 1 00
Poems of M. Grecourt, 2 do. 25
Court Register, 6 do. 12mo. 1 50
6 Pamphlets, Political Journal, (in German,) 50
Description of a Monument, 1 vol. 50

	$	cts
Beacon Hill, 1 vol.		25
Letters in the English and German Language, 1 do.		25
A Family Housekeeper, 1 do.		25
Pamphlets of different descriptions	15	00

Maps, Charts, &c.

	$	cts
Chart of Navigation from the Gulf of Honda to Philadelphia, by Hamilton Moore, ———————————— to Bay of Fundy, do.	40	00
Griffith's Map of Pennsylvania and Sketch of Delaware	8	00
Howell's large Map of Pennsylvania	10	00
Henry's Map of Virginia	8	00
Bradley's Map of the United States	5	00
Holland's Map of New Hampshire	3	00
Ellicott's Map of the West End of Lake Ontario	4	00
Hutchins's Map of the Western Part of Virginia, Maryland, Pennsylvania, and North Carolina	3	00
Adlum and Williams's Map of Pennsylvania	2	00
Map of Kennebec River, &c.	1	00
Andrews's Military Map of the Seat of War in the Netherlands	1	00
Howell's small Map of Pennsylvania	2	00
Great Canal between Forth and Clyde	2	00
Plan of the Line between North Carolina and Virginia	2	00
M'Murray's Map of the United States	3	00
Military Plans of the American Revolution	8	00
Evans's Map of Pennsylvania, New Jersey, New York, and Delaware	1	00
Plan of the Mississippi from the River Iberville to the River Yazoo	2	00

	$	cts
Map of India	5	00
Chart of France	1	00
Map of the World		50
Map of the State of Connecticut	2	00
Spanish Maps		50
Table of Commerce and Population of France		50
Battle of the Nile, &c.	1	00
Routes and Order of Battle of Generals St. Clair and Harmer	1	00
Truxtun on the Rigging of a Frigate	1	00
View of the Encampment of West Point		50
Emblematic Prints	4	00
Plan of the Government House of New York		50
Chase and Action between the Constellation and Insurgent, (2 prints,)	4	00
General Wilkinson's Map of Part of the Western Territory	1	00
Plan of Mount Vernon by John Vaughan	1	00
Specimen of Penmanship		50
5 Plans of the Federal City and District	5	00
1 Large Draught	3	00
Plan of the City of New York Panopticon		80
Hoop's Map of the State of New York	1	00
Howell's Pocket Map of the State of Pennsylvania	2	00
A French Map of the Carolinas	2	00
Fry and Jefferson's Map of Virginia	2	00
Howell's small Map of Pennsylvania	2	00
A Map of New England	2	00
9 Maps of different Parts of Virginia and Carolina, and also a Number of loose Maps	52	00
Carlton's Map (2 sets) of the Coasts of North America	8	00
Treatise on Cavalry, with large Cuts	50	00

	$	cts.
Walker's View in Scotland	3	0C
A large Portfolio with sundry Engravings	40	00
Alexander's Victories, 26 prints	100	00
8 Reams of large folio Paper	40	00
2 Reams of small Paper	8	00
13 Reams of Letter Paper	39	00
5 Whole Packages of Sealingwax	5	00
5 Leaden Paper Presses	5	00
6 Blank Books	18	00
13 Small Books	2	00
1 Large Globe	50	00
1 Trunk	6	00

Books omitted.

Dictionary of Arts and Sciences, 4 vols. 8vo.	20	00
Smollet's History of England, 1 do.	11	00
Handmaid to the Arts, 2 do.	2	00
Bancroft on Permanent Colors, 1 do.	1	00

1 Theodolite	50	00

*   *   *   *   *   *

Plate belonging to Mount Vernon.

44 lbs. 15 oz.	900	00

Plated Ware.

2 Bottle Stands	2	00
1 Large Waiter	8	00
2 Waiters, 2d size	6	00
4 Waiters	8	00
1 Bread Basket	8	00
1 Fish Knife	2	00
6 Salt Stands	12	00
4 Bottle Sliders	4	00

		$	cts
1 Coffee Urn		8	00
1 Tea Urn		20	00
4 Pair of high Candlesticks		40	00
3 Pair of Chamber Candlesticks		9	00
1 Set of Casters		20	00
2 Cream Dishes		6	00
2 Sugar Dishes		8	00
2 Mustard-pots		4	00
7 Salts		17	00
Wine Strainer		1	50
1 Cream-pot		3	00
1 Snuffer Stand		1	00
1 Muffin Dish		3	00
1 Tea Urn		50	00
2 Pair of high Candlesticks		30	00
1 Pair of small Candlesticks		3	00
1 Lamp		10	00
1 Bread Basket		10	00
1 Ladle			50
1 Pair of large Coolers		60	00
2 Pair of small Coolers		60	00
1 Waiter		10	00

*   *   *   *   *   *

Sum total ·$27,158 34

The whole number of Negroes left by General Washington, in his own right, is as follows:—

Men	40
Women	37
Working Boys	4
Working Girls	3
Children	40
Total	124

whom Mrs. Washington intending to liberate at the end of the present year, can only be valued for the service of the working negroes for one year.*

	$	cts.
Amount brought forward	27,158	34
Books omitted, and a Theodolite	84	00
Stock	29,212	00
Cash on hand	254	70
Diamond Eagle	387	00
Addition to Buckles	200	00
	$57,296	04

In obedience to the annexed order of Court, we, the subscribers, being duly sworn, have viewed and appraised all the personal property of the late General George Washington, deceased, which was presented to us for that purpose, agreeably to the foregoing schedule.

Signed by   THOMSON MASON,
TOBIAS LEAR,
THOMAS PETER,
WM. H. FOOTE.

NOTE.

A great many of the titles of the books in the foregoing inventory are very imperfectly, some of them very inaccurately given. Most of these errors probably existed in the original appraisement. Of several of them the correction was obvious; others have been corrected conjecturally; but for want of means to restore the true reading, others have been necessarily left, as they stand in the copy of the inventory furnished for this work.

---

* No valuation of this item is carried out in the Inventory.

No. III.

[The interest which attaches to everything connected with Mount Vernon, has led to the insertion of the following copy of the Will of Mrs. Washington, which, it is believed, has never before been printed. It was kindly furnished from the office of the Clerk of Fairfax County, by Mr. Thomas Moore.]

THE WILL OF MARTHA WASHINGTON OF MOUNT VERNON.

In the name of GOD, *Amen.*

I, MARTHA WASHINGTON, of Mount Vernon, in the County of Fairfax, being of sound mind and capable of disposing of my worldly estate, do make, ordain, and declare this to be my last Will and Testament, hereby revoking all other wills and testaments by me heretofore made.

Imprimis.—It is my desire that all my just debts may be punctually paid, and that as speedily as the same can be done.

Item.—I give and devise to my nephew, Bartholomew Dandridge, and his heirs, my lot in the town of Alexandria, situate on Pitt and Cameron Streets, devised to me by my late husband, George Washington, deceased.

Item.—I give and bequeath to my four nieces, Martha W. Dandridge, Mary Dandridge, Frances Lucy Dandridge, and Frances Henley, the debt of two thousand pounds due from Lawrence Lewis and secured by his bond, to be equally divided between them or such of them as shall be alive at my death, and to be paid to them respectively on the days of their respective marriage or arrival at the age of twenty-one years, whichsoever shall first happen, together with all the interest on said debt remaining unpaid at the time of my death; and in case the whole or any part of the said principal sum of two thousand pounds shall be paid to me during my life, then it is my will that so much money be raised out of my estate as shall be equal to what I shall have received of the said principal debt, and distributed among my four nieces aforesaid as herein has been bequeathed; and it is my meaning that the interest accruing after my death on the said sum of two thousand pounds shall belong to my said nieces, and be equally divided between them or such of them as shall be alive at the time of my death, and be paid annually for their respective uses, until they receive their shares of the principal.

Item.—I give and bequeath to my grandson, George Washington Parke Custis, all the silver plate of every kind of which I shall die possessed, together with the two large plated coolers, the four small plated coolers, with the bottle casters, and a pipe of wine, if there be one in the house at the time of my death; also the set of Cincinnati tea and table china, the bowl that has a —— in it, the fine old china jars which usually stand on the chimney-piece in the new room; also all the family pictures of every sort and the pictures painted by his sister, and two small screens worked one by his sister and the other a present from Miss Kitty Brown, also his choice of prints; also the two girandoles and lustres that stand on them; also the new bedstead which I caused to be made in Philadelphia, together with the bed, mattress, bolsters, and pillows, and the white dimity curtains belonging thereto; also two other beds with bolsters and pillows, and the white dimity window-curtains in the new room; also the iron chest and the desk in my closet which belonged to my first husband; also all my books of every kind except the large Bible and prayer-book; also the set of tea china that was given me by Mr. Van Braam, every piece having M. W. on it.

Item.—I give and bequeath to my grand-daughter, Martha Peter, my writing-table and the seat to it standing in my chamber, also the print of General Washington that hangs in the passage.

Item.—I give and bequeath to my grand-daughter, Elizabeth Parke Law, the dressing-table and glass that stands in the chamber called the yellow room, and General Washington's picture painted by Trumbull.

Item.—I give and bequeath to my grand-daughter, Eleanor Parke Lewis, the large looking-glass in the front parlour and any other looking-glass which she may choose; also one of the new sideboard tables in the new room; also twelve chairs with green bottoms to be selected by herself; also the marble table in the garret; also the two prints of the Dead Soldier, a print of the Washington family in a box in the garret, and the great chair standing in my chamber; also all the plated ware not hereinbefore otherwise bequeathed; also all the sheets, table-linen, napkins, towels, pillow-cases remaining in the house at my death; also three beds and bedsteads, curtains, bolsters, and pillows for each bed such as she shall choose, and not herein particularly otherwise bequeathed, together with counterpanes and a pair of blankets for each bed; also all the wineglasses and decanters of every kind, and all the blue and white china in common use.

Item.—It is my will and desire that all the wine in bottles in the vaults be equally divided between my grand-daughters and grandson, to each of whom I bequeath ten guineas to buy a ring for each.

Item.—It is my will and desire that Anna Maria Washington, the daughter of my niece, be put into handsome mourning at my death, at the expense of my estate; and I bequeath to her ten guineas to buy a ring.

Item.—I give and bequeath to my neighbor, Mrs. Elizabeth Washington, five guineas to get something in remembrance of me.

Item.—I give and bequeath to Mrs. David Stuart five guineas to buy her a ring.

Item.—I give and bequeath to Benjamin Lincoln Lear one hundred pounds specie, to be vested in funded stock of the United States immediately after my decease, and to stand in his name as his property, which investment my executors are to cause to be made.

Item.—When the vestry of Truro parish shall buy a glebe, I devise, will, and bequeath that my executors shall pay one hundred pounds to them in aid of the purchase, provided the said purchase be made in my lifetime or within three years after my decease.

Item.—It is my will and desire that all the rest and residue of my estate of whatever kind and description, not herein specifically devised or bequeathed, shall be sold by the executors of this my last will for ready money, as soon after my decease as the same can be done, and that the proceeds thereof together with all the money in the house and the debts due to me (the debts due from me and the legacies herein bequeathed being first satisfied) shall be invested by my executors in eight per cent. stock of the funds of the United States, and shall stand on the books in the name of my executors in their character of executors of my will; and it is my desire that the interest thereof shall be applied to the proper education of Bartholomew Henley and Samuel Henley, the two youngest sons of my sister Henley, and also to the education of John Dandridge, son of my deceased nephew John Dandridge, so that they may be severally fitted and accomplished in some useful trade; and to each of them who shall have lived to finish his education, or to reach the age of twenty-one years, I give and bequeath one hundred pounds to set him up in his trade.

Item.— My debts and legacies being paid, and the education of Bartholomew Henley, Samuel Henley, and John Dandridge aforesaid being completed, or they being all dead before the completion thereof, it is my will and desire that all my estates and interests in whatever form existing, whether in money, funded stock, or any other species of property, shall be equally divided among all the persons hereinafter named, who shall be living at the time that the interest of the funded stock shall cease to be applicable, in pursuance of my will hereinbefore expressed, to the education of my nephews, Bartholomew Henley, Samuel Henley, and John Dandridge, namely, among Anna Maria Washington, daughter of my niece, and John Dandridge, son of my nephew, and all my great-grandchildren living at the time that the interest of the said funded stock shall cease to be applicable to the education of the said B. Henley, S. Henley, and John Dandridge, and the interest shall cease to be so applied when all of them shall die before they arrive to the age of twenty-one years, or those living shall have finished their education or have arrived to the age of twenty-one years, and so long as any one of the three lives who has not finished his education or arrived to the age of twenty-one years, the division of the said residuum is to be deferred, and no longer.

Lastly, I nominate and appoint my grandson, George Washington Parke Custis, my nephews, Julius B. Dandridge and Bartholomew Dandridge, and my son-in-law, Thomas Peter, executors of this my last will and testament.

In witness whereof I have hereunto set my hand and seal this twenty-second day of September, in the year eighteen hundred.

MARTHA WASHINGTON [seal]

Sealed, signed, acknowledged and delivered as her last will and testament, in the presence of us the subscribing witnesses, who have been requested to subscribe the same as such in her presence.

ROGER FARRELL,
WILLIAM SPENCE,
LAWRENCE LEWIS,
MARTHA PETER.

March 4th, 1802.*

I give to my grandson, George Washington Parke Custis, my mulatto man Elish, that I bought of Mr. Butler Washington, to him and his heirs forever.

M. WASHINGTON.

At a Court held for Fairfax County the 21st day of June, 1802, —

This last will and testament of Martha Washington, deceased, was presented in Court by George Washington Parke Custis and Thomas Peter, two of the executors therein named, who made oath thereto, and the same being proved by the oaths of Roger Farrell, William Spence, and Lawrence Lewis, three of the subscribing witnesses thereto, is, together with a codicil or memorandum indorsed thereon, ordered to be recorded, and the said executors having performed what the law requires, a certificate is granted them for obtaining a probate thereof in due form.

Teste

WM. MOSS, Cl.

A copy,

Teste

THOMAS MOORE, D. C.

* Mrs. Washington died on the 22d of May, 1802.

INDEX.

A.

Account-Book, Washington's, as Commander-in-chief, autograph, 111. Lithographed, in facsimile, 111.

Acute laryngitis, the disease of which Washington died, 275. See *Inflammation*.

ADAMS, JOHN, proposes Washington to Congress as Commander-in-chief, 110. Chosen first Vice-President of the United States, 171. Nominates Washington as Commander-in-chief in the prospect of a war with France, 230.

AMES, FISHER, his celebrated speech in Congress on Jay's Treaty, 199.

ANDRÉ, JOHN, his condemnation and execution as a spy, 144, 145.

Annapolis, Washington resigns his commission to Congress in session there, 150–153.

Army, Continental, its wretched condition at the beginning of the Revolution, 112–114.

ARNOLD, BENEDICT, his treason discovered by Washington, 144.

Articles at Mount Vernon, Inventory of, with their appraised value annexed, 286–317.

---

* This Index was prepared, at Mr. Everett's request, by CHARLES FOLSOM, Esq., of Cambridge.

C.

D.

G.

H.

near New York, 117. Reinforced by Clinton and Cornwallis, 117. Enters Philadelphia, 132.

HUMBOLDT, ALEXANDER, his death a loss to science and letters, ix.

Hunting Creek, the original name of Mount Vernon, 38.

I.

Inflammation of the larynx, the disease of which Washington died, 275. Nature of the disease, 275–279. Its treatment, 279 *et seq.* Dr. Baillie's method, 280. Dr. Watson's, 280. Treatment of it by Washington's physicians justified, 284.

Iron chest, contents of Washington's, at Mt. Vernon, 295, 296.

IRVING, WASHINGTON, his "Life of Washington," commended, ii. 27.

J.

JACKSON, DR. JAMES, his Memoir on the last sickness of Washington, 273–285.

JAY, JOHN, special minister to England, 195. His treaty, and its unpopularity, 195 *et seq.*

JEFFERSON, THOMAS, first Secretary of State, 178. Leader of one of the two great political parties, 181. Retires from the Cabinet, 183.

JUMONVILLE, a French leader, killed at Great Meadows, 68. Not "assassinated," 71.

K.

KING, RUFUS, his testimony to the English estimate of Washington's character, 263.

M.

N.

O.

P.

R.

S.

T.

ence of his character throughout the country, 162. Appointed President of the Federal Convention which framed the Constitution of the United States, 167. Unanimously chosen President of the United States, 171. Pays a farewell visit to his mother, 174. Her maternal commendation of him, 174. Repairs to New York, the first seat of government, 172. Takes the oath of office, 172. Organizes his cabinet, 178. Makes a tour through the Eastern States, 185. Enters on his second term of office, unanimously reëlected, 187. Proclaims neutrality in relation to France and Great Britain, 191. Represses the insolence of Genet, 192. Appoints Mr. Jay special minister to England, 195. His firmness under the unpopularity of Jay's treaty, 198. Refuses to communicate his instructions to Mr. Jay from constitutional principle, 198–204. Quells the insurrection in Pennsylvania, 205–207. Solicits the liberation of Lafayette, 209. His kindness to the family of Lafayette, 209–211. His " Farewell Address," its origin and composition, 211–222. Affecting circumstances of his farewell dinner as President, 223, 224. His last official letter, denouncing the forged correspondence, 225. Retires to Mount Vernon, and resumes his agricultural pursuits, 226. Accepts the appointment of commander-in-chief of the armies of the United States in an impending war with France, 231. His last illness, 237–249. His last words, 247. Funeral honors, and manifestations of public sorrow at his departure, 249–250. His last will, 251. His disposition of his property, and provision for the emancipation and care of his slaves, 252–257. Inventory of his personal property at Mount Vernon, 286–317. His personal appearance in harmony with his character, 258. His personal habits, temperament, and social qualities, 259, 260. His religious

9 783337 056353